DEATH OF LADY MACDEATH

WYLD ENCHANTMENT WOODS
COZY MYSTERY

Kura Jane Carpenter

WUP
Wicked Unicorn Press

Dedication:
To **Alice & Lynn**

~ And the legend
that was 'fat soap'

Published by **Wicked Unicorn Press**

National Library of New Zealand Cataloguing-in-Publication Data
Death of Lady MacDeath / Kura Jane Carpenter
softcover ISBN 978-1-0670080-1-7

MAP OF ELLA'S HOME

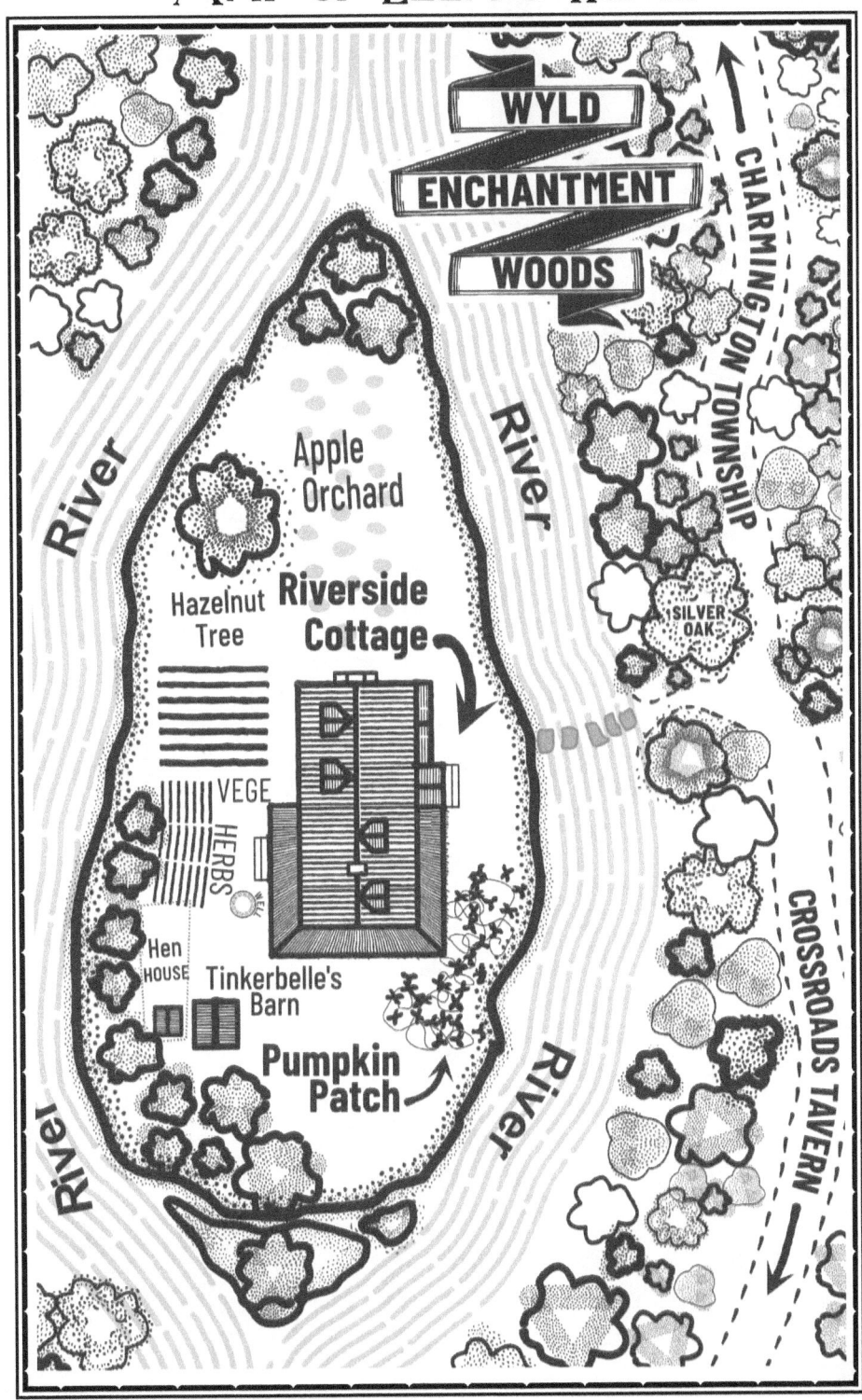

WYLD ENCHANTMENT WOODS

CHARMINGTON TOWNSHIP

River

Apple Orchard

Hazelnut Tree

Riverside Cottage

SILVER OAK

VEGE

HERBS

Hen HOUSE

Tinkerbelle's Barn

Pumpkin Patch

River

CROSSROADS TAVERN

CONTENTS

CAST OF CHARACTERS

- **Ella Charming** – our delightful mystery-solving protagonist.
- **Tom April** – Rookie Guardsman - Accidentally swapped bodies with Ella's cat.
- Axel Luther – Sheriff. Former Captain of the Castle guards.
- Bertram Spalding – Mayoral candidate, Wife Catherine, son Charles.
- Bethany – child with strong wyld magic, granddaughter of Betty.
- Betty – Owner of Betty's Pies on Hot Cockle Lane.
- Bob and Fishstix – Actors belonging to the Pickford Players.
- Bron the Baker – Baker, suspected werewolf.
- Cassidy Turpin – Guardswoman, on the night watch – Niece of Dirk.
- (Charles) Spalding – Actor, member of Pickford Players.
- Cheapcuts / Chelton Junior – Son of Martha and Chelton.
- Chelton – Butcher – Husband of Martha.
- Claude – Actor from Avalon, now runs a bookshop. Mayoral candidate.
- Cinderella (deceased) – Princess – Sister of Ella and Sibylla.
- Dirk Turpin – Royal coachman – Uncle of Cassidy Turpin.
- Docter Edison Hyde – runs the charity hosptial on Hot Cockle Lane.
- Goldilocks – Royal hairdresser, former magical healer.
- Gretel – Vampire – Sister of Hansel.
- Hansel – Vampire – Brother of Gretel.
- Harold Harper – Former Postmaster, Mayoral candidate.
- Hillary Harper – Former Post office clerk – Daughter of Harold.
- Jacob Marley – Accountant. Mayoral candidate.
- Marge – Midwife – A notorious gossip.
- Martha Chelton – Wife of Chelton the butcher.
- Master Spicer – Cook at the Nottingham Home for Unwanted Boys.
- Merlin – Famous Magician – Ella's brother, lives in Avalon.
- Mistress Lily Fairweather – Matron of the Baker Street orphanage.
- Mr Beau – Shoe shine man and Lamplighter.
- Mr Puddles – Willow's pet poodle.
- Mrs Haversham – Former headmistress of the Haversham Academy.
- Nigella Pickford – Actress and director.
- Olly May – Ward of Sally, former orphan/pickpocket.
- Peach and Perry – Horses that pull the royal carriage.
- Pickford Players – An acting troop under Nigella.
- Prince John – Regent of Sherwood.
- Richard – Husband of Cinderella.
- Robinne Scarlett – Brewer at the Crossroads Tavern, suspected rebel.
- Rooster – A Nottingham criminal.
- Sally Mercer – Haberdashery owner.
- Sam and Sandy – Orphan children with Wyld Magic.
- Sibylla – Queen of Wyld Kingdom – Twin sister of Ella.
- Tilly – Ella's cat.
- Willow – Baker and Witch – A newcomer to Charmington.
- Wulf – Bodyguard to Prince John.

CHAPTER 1

THE VOW

Where had that cat run off to? Ella wondered as she stood on the porch of her neat little cottage. Across the snow-covered lawn, by the edge of the frozen river, something was stirring within the pumpkin patch. Of course. Tomcat had been all but sleeping out there for the last week, tending the giant pumpkin in which his human body lay encased in a magical stasis.

Walking stick in hand, Ella shuffled over, her boots crunching on the snow, she breathed in the crisp winter air, sharp with the scent of pine. The pumpkin vines dipped and swayed. Some reached out to pet her, their rough leaves rasping against the wool of her cloak and dusting her face with ice. "Oh!" Annoyed, Ella pushed the fronds aside and called to Tom, who, as she suspected, was curled in a white cat ball atop his broad six-foot 'pumpkin egg', as he called it.

"I have to go into Charmington this morning," she said, adjusting her gloves. "I have an appointment with Hansel. You may come along if you want. But I expect it will be very boring..."

She let the words hang. It wasn't as she wanted Tom's company. Or that she was worrying about him. Night after night staring out the pumpkin...

"... Hansel has been combing through the post office's accounting books for the past few weeks, trying to uncover what Harold was hiding."

Tomcat's ears perked up. "The fake set of ledgers that Harold was keeping?"

Ella nodded. "Indeed."

"Do you think Harold was stealing money?" Tomcat's fluffy tail stood straight. "Ooh! Maybe if he didn't spend it? Maybe he's been hoarding it? If Hansel can track down what happened to it, will it help solve the kingdom's financial problems?"

Ella bit her lip. The very same thought had crossed her mind a time or two—especially in the early hours when she lay awake fretting. To think their kingdom was so close to financial ruin that they might have to accept Prince John of Sherwood's request and allow him to rent out land in Wyld Enchantment Woods on which to build a prison. What a dreadful notion. "Regardless of how much Harold embezzled, it will take a long time to restore all the kingdom's finances."

Tomcat blinked and regarded Ella with his—or rather, with her cat Tilly's—sparkling green cat eyes. "I'm sure you'll figure it out—I have faith in you. You're very clever."

Ella allowed herself a moment of pleasure at Tom's words. "And you are very kind."

He shrugged. "That's just what friends do. Support each other."

Friends... To think that a few months ago she had barely a friend in the world—no. That wasn't true. She had shut out and pushed her friends away. It was Tom entering her life and forcing her to mix again with the Charmington population that had reminded her she had many friends, if she would only accept their help.

If only she could help Tom—restore him to his human form, repay his kindness—but alas, no...

Ella's thoughts drifted to the useless wand on her mantelpiece inside—snapped in two when she was stripped of her powers years ago for breaking the Fairy Godmother rules...

...Without her magic, she couldn't do anything to speed Tom's recovery...

Ella glanced up at the sound of footsteps. Their neighbour Robinne approached across the frozen-over creek, footfall padding on the ice. "Good morning," Robinne called, lowering the hood of her red woollen cloak. Her pretty face creased with a frown. "Um...today's the last day, right?"

Tomcat slid off the pumpkin, shaking snow and plant matter from his fur. "Yes, I know about Cass leaving tomorrow, but I didn't want to worry Ella."

Ella blanched. Cassidy had rather an eventful time in the last two months. Had something unfortunate befallen her yet again? She worked on the Charmington night's watch—and though he did his best to keep his feelings to himself, wary to confess how he felt when he was trapped in a cat's body, Ella knew Tom was completely enraptured with the capable young lady. "Is Cassidy all right?"

Tom's tail sagged. "You know how Cass's cousin Bethany has been offered a full scholarship to attend that magical academy in Avalon?"

Ella had assumed as much after her awful show-off of a brother, Merlin, had whirled into town last month, as did he now and then, upsetting everything, making a fool of himself and then swanning off again. "Bethany's wyld magic was exceptionally strong. I suggested Merlin offer her a scholarship to that school he *supposedly* lectures at, but she's very young. Surely Bethany wouldn't be old enough to attend yet?"

Robinne took up the story. "Apparently, they are desperate to sign Bethany up before another academy can claim her, so they're supporting the whole family to move."

Ella was shocked. "What? The *entire* family? But...but..."

"Cassidy will love Avalon," Tomcat said stoically, and he puffed out his chest in what Ella had learned he did when he was trying to make the best of things. "They've even lined up an exciting job for her at the Academy as a bodyguard so she can stay close to Bethany. They will both thrive there."

I wish I could go with her...

Tomcat didn't say the words aloud, but Ella could guess what he was thinking, because once, long ago, she had been in the same place. In love with someone but too afraid to tell them. Afraid to risk ruining their friendship. What would she do now—if she had that chance again?

Ella's eyes stung, and she swallowed down a tear. "Have you told Cassidy how you feel about her? Maybe she would stay."

Tom opened his mouth as if to protest, but then just shook his head.

"See!" Robinne said, down to the cat. "Didn't I say the exact same thing to you? If you don't tell Cassidy how you feel, then she's going to leave."

Tomcat cut a paw through the air. "I appreciate what you're both saying. But it wouldn't be fair to her." He waved a hand at his furry body. "I'm a cat. Not a man. It would be *weird*—and besides. It would be *wrong* to put any pressure on her to stay—even if I was still human. I want Cassidy to go to Avalon—to become an elite guardswoman, or whatever she chooses. I want her to live *her* dreams, not mine." He took a breath. "If you truly love something, let it go."

"Fine, do what you feel is best," Robinne said, shrugging a bag she was carrying off her shoulder. "I've got those spare clothes you wanted for Wulf. Where did you want them?"

"In the barn, thank you, my dear."

Robinne wandered off to place the clothes in the donkey barn, but not before Robinne and Ella exchanged glances. My goodness. Tom truly was an extraordinary young man. He may be trapped in a cat's body, but he was the kindest, most gallant soul she had ever encountered.

An idea popped into Ella's head. Though *her* wand was broken, she had a *friend* whose wand was still intact. *Goldilocks!*

Though Goldilocks was now the queen's hairdresser, Goldi had once been a powerful magical healer. And, despite the queen's ban on magic, Goldi dabbled now and then when no one was looking. "You have given me an idea, Tom. Though my wand can't restore you, Goldi's wand is fully functional—"

"Ella! That's a brilliant idea!" Tom's eyes went wide and his fur stood on end. "You think Goldi can use her wand to fix *your* wand?"

Ella blinked. No. That wasn't what she thought at all. What a peculiar suggestion. Use a magic wand to *fix* a broken magic wand? "No, it would take a full pardon and the power from the Fairy Council to restore *my* wand—they were the ones that bound and stripped my powers." Ella sighed. It was up to the council to undo what they had wrought... "I just meant Goldi might be able to help *you* return to your *human* form. I don't want you to get your hopes up, but healing is—was—Goldi's speciality."

Tomcat's whiskers vibrated. "Hopes up! Hopes up!" he said, dancing about the snow-dusted pumpkin patch and darting through the foliage. The magical pumpkin vines coiled and swayed around the little white cat.

"No, Tom!" Ella sighed, hands on hips. "I said, *don't* get your hopes up." But secretly she smiled. He always looked on the bright side. Despite all that had happened, he never gave up.

Ella clenched her bony fists. Magic preserve! That a kind and helpful soul like Tom was trapped like this—it wasn't just unfair, it was unjust! So maybe she didn't have her magical powers any more, but Tom had taught her she did have friends. It was about time she put aside her pride and asked for their help!

"Tom April, you are my friend," Ella said aloud, and she shook with indignation. "Of anyone I have met, you deserve your chance at happiness. Justice must prevail! Whatever it takes! By the end of today, we will find out how to restore you back to your human body! This I vow!"

CHAPTER 2

STRANGER DANGER

NORTHGATE SQUARE, CHARMINGTON.

Ella, Robinne, and Tomcat walked through the old iron town gates and onto the cobblestones of Northgate Square. In the distance, their destination, Charmington's grand town hall, waited, pleasantly familiar with the domed slate roof under its perpetual coating of snow, the lead glass diamonds black in the early light, as the tall clock tower chimed out the hour.

Less familiar were a dozen or more roguish looking strangers. Most wore hunter green and carried crossbows or other hunting gear. Some loitered by the noticeboard outside the police station, while others lingered on the town steps.

"That's odd. Why so many strangers…?" Robinne narrowed her eyes at the unfamiliar faces, and dread coiled in Ella's stomach.

Ella winced and leaned on her walking stick. "Could this be Sheriff Axel's doing?"

Last month, the sheriff had threatened to post a reward to capture cats. Had he stayed true to his word? Was he actually determined to capture random cats in the misguided attempt to also net Tomcat?

"I think it's just because the ice barge has just arrived from Nottingham," Tomcat suggested, seemingly oblivious to any personal dangers. "It stops overnight before it travels on to Avalon tomorrow." He sighed and muttered something about Cassidy leaving on it, and making lots of new—undoubtedly handsome—friends on her journey.

Robinne scooped him into her arms so the trio could chat more comfortably without making it obvious they were having a conversation with a cat and they all surveyed the unfamiliar faces with suspicion.

Tomcat blinked up at the town hall's attic rooms nestled under the snowy slate roof, high above the square. "Are you meeting Hansel in your tax office?" he whispered, a sympathetic tone in his voice. "I can ask him to come downstairs and we'll find another meeting place rather than the attic. Since your knees are sore, I'm sure you won't want to walk up all the steps."

"You are kind, but no. I am meeting Hansel in the post office on the ground floor. Since Harold was removed from his position as postmaster, I no longer desire to avoid the place. It is a lovely building, after all, and as Hansel is investigating the accounts ledgers of the post office, I thought it would make sense to discuss matters there..."

"Hey, when you go ask Goldi to use her magic to change Tom back," Robinne interjected, her breath fanning out on the crisp mountain morning air, "you should get your knees done at the same time. You said Goldi had a temporary pain relief spell, right?"

Ella nodded. "Indeed. Repeated flights up and down the stairs in my duty as the tax collector has certainly increased the discomfort from my arthritis. I would be foolish to continue to ignore it..." She gestured for them to carry on now that she had had a moment to rest, when Tom wriggled from Robinne's grasp and leapt to the ground.

"Look! Olly and Sally are waving at us!"

They looked up at the second-floor window of the haberdashery building across the square where the elderly milliner and her young ward were frantically making T shapes with their hands. "I think they want you, Tom."

"I'll catch up with you later," Tom said, prancing off, his white paw leaving little dents in the snow.

Ella thought about yelling at him, "Don't talk to strangers!" But that was hardly advisable.

"He's fast," Robinne said, with a shrug. "The sheriff will never catch him."

"I hope not... Life would be dull without him..." In the months Tom had lived as Tomcat under her roof, Ella hadn't had to face any danger or fears alone. He was a loyal friend. In many respects, she had begun to hope he would always be with her. She dreaded the thought of living alone deep in Wyld Enchantment Woods again once they restored him to his human form. But it was like Tom had said, if you loved something, there came a time you must let it go. "Shall we..."

Together they wandered past the rearing Unicorn statue set in the middle of a frozen water fountain and up the steps at the foot of the town hall and post office building.

Suddenly, the post office's wooden doors banged open. A burly man was flung out from the building.

He tumbled down the snowy steps, cursing as he did so, but dressed in a heavy tunic and cloak he seemed unhurt, and was on his feet a second later—running for his life. Boots pounded away across the cobbles.

In the post office doorway, a snarling young girl of about eight years old appeared, clutching a crossbow. Gretel.

"Can't you read?" Gretel shouted in her German-tinged accent at the fleeing man. "No crossbows in post office!" She snapped the crossbow over the knee of her denim dirndl skirt, chucked the broken weapon to the flagstones and swept a yellow pigtail over her shoulder. Gretel's little white fangs protruded as she hissed, the daylight catching her face. She stepped back into the doorway shadow, pointed to a new hand-painted sign that spelled out: *Leave weapons outside, dummkopf!*

"Gracious!" Startled, Ella and Robinne came up short. "Whatever is going on?"

"Fortune hunters!" Gretel spat, and then pointed at Robinne. "You! I need a bouncer. Make sure stupid hunters leave veapons." She kicked a cardboard box left by the door for that purpose, with the toe of her distinctive yellow duckie boots. "You vork, I pay good vages."

Robinne exchanged glances with Ella and shrugged an apology. "I could do with the money..."

Ella only nodded. *Couldn't they all.* Charmington's fortunes had long faded.

Especially with magic being banned again after the brief magical amnesty that her twin sister Queen Sibylla had allowed temporarily last month during Merlin's promotional book tour to the township. Hopefully, Hansel had some good news to report. It wasn't as if there was anything of value wandering around freely, waiting to be scooped up or pounced on.

"Highness," Gretel muttered, dusting her little hands and smoothing her dirndl skirt, seemingly her mood improved, "Hansel is expecting. Come, come..."

"Wait, Ella," Robinne said, grabbing Ella's arm. "Don't forget, last month you promised to let me know if a mystery or a murder pops up. I don't want to miss out again on being there for the cool bit when you figure out who the bad guys are."

Ella rolled her eyes. "Magic preserve. Mystery? What mystery? I am confident today will be spent investigating dry account books."

Gracious, the young were always so quick to let their imaginations run away with them. She left Robinne on the doorstep and followed the little vampire inside the post office, and called back over her shoulder, "There certainly won't be any murders!"

GRETEL USHERED ELLA A CIRCUIT through the public foyer area of the grand old building and then into the offices where the postal workers' polished wooden desks were lined up in efficient rows. "Vait, please, I fetch Hansel from zee basement."

Ella nodded and leaned on her cane. She briefly cast a glance at an oil painting of her sister Queen Sibylla. The official royal portrait was hung in such a way as to cast a regal gaze at her subjects, all industrially working below. Former postmaster Harold Harper's own self-important portrait had been removed, and now the walls were hung with large posters featuring the mayoral candidate hopefuls. She had forgotten that a new mayor was to be elected following the unfortunate poisoning of the former mayor last month.

The former Mayor, Sebastian, had held the position for many years and there was speculation that his son, Bertram, would follow in his father's footsteps—a shoo-in for winning the vote. Despite this supposedly foregone conclusion, there were several candidates vying for public attention judging from the number of posters. Ella studied the posters.

As expected, she recognised many of the names of the prospective candidates. No wonder, considering the length of time she had lived in Wyld Kingdom. That notion had her wonderings return to the unusual increase in strangers wandering around outside the police station and the one Gretel had thrown out of the post office.

What in the world had drawn fortune hunters to Charmington? Certainly, back in the day, magic had lured many such people to their kingdom, but that was many years ago... Charmington's fortunes had faded—indeed, that was her purpose for being here. To meet Hansel and hear several reports about the state of the town, including the financial report that Hansel had prepared around the fake post office account books they discovered being kept by the former postmaster Harold Harper.

At that moment Gretel waved and gestured over to where her brother Hansel had appeared at the top of a small staircase that connected the office area to the vast basement storage that ran under the post office and warren of town hall buildings.

Though Ella had told Tomcat not to get his hopes up, Ella realised she expected Hansel would reveal Harold stole *lots* of money. Even better, hopefully they could prove it and get most of it back to help restore the town's finances. Surely that wasn't too much to hope for?

CHAPTER 3

HANSEL HAS BAD NEWS, BEAU HAS WORSE

HANSEL DASHED ELLA'S HOPES INSTANTLY.

"Highness." He bowed in greeting, snapped his heels together and gestured for Ella to sit with him at his desk. "Zere is good news and bad news," he said, pulling out a chair for her in front of a tidy desktop with carefully laid out ledgers and assorted ink pots and pens. He brushed his hand through his blond hair with a sigh. He sounded many years older than his youthful outward appearance of a twelve year boy would suggest—which was true, Hansel and his sister Gretel were the town's oldest inhabitants, even older than Ella and her twin sister, Queen Sibylla, who had lived in Charmington for hundreds of years.

"Bad news first," Ella said, settling into the leather chair and breathing in the familiar lemon-scented wood polish that saturated every gleaming surface within the post office. "Proceed. Tell me how much Harold stole. I am braced."

Hansel patted the leather-bound green ledger on the desktop in front of him. One of the ledgers that Ella and Tom had uncovered, hidden in the basement two months ago. "Harold vas not stealing money from zee post office. Zat is actually zee *gut* news."

Ella blinked. "Wait. What? He *wasn't* stealing money?" Ella's hopes perked up. Did that mean their finances weren't as bad as her sister Sibylla had implied? "But then...what was the purpose of a fake set of ledgers?"

"Harold Harper *vasn't* stealing or embezzling money." Hansel cocked his head to the side. "Instead, he vas going to a lot of effort to cover up zat zee post office vas *losing* money."

"Harold was trying to make the finances appear *better* than they were?" Ella struggled to comprehend what Hansel was telling her. "Whatever for?"

Hansel's lips pushed out in a shrug and he hooked his hands under the straps of his lederhosen. "Perhaps to maintain a facade of respectability?"

Ella closed her eyes, sinking deeper into the chair. Oh dear. That was the good news? "And how bad is it?"

Hansel flipped open another ledger and pointed to rows of his own neat handwriting and figures tallied. Rows and rows of numbers, all written in red. "Like our kingdom, zee post office is in deep financial straits and on zee verge of bankruptcy."

Ella found she'd pressed her forehead to the surface of the desk and she lifted her head before any of the workers saw. *Hold your head high and carry on* was Ella's motto. "I see."

"Vould you like to hear zee bad news now?" Hansel enquired politely.

A hollow pit of despair bloomed across Ella's narrow chest. Verge of bankruptcy *wasn't* the bad news? She swallowed and nodded, bracing herself for the answer.

"To pinch zee pennies, Harold trimmed as many expenses as possible..."

Ella felt a momentary surge of hope.

"...including even *necessary* expenses. He had zee maintenance crews fired two years ago."

Ella was shocked. "The post office has had no maintenance work for *two* years? But this is a large public building!"

Hansel held up a finger to stay her words. "Not just zee post office. Harold vas in charge of appointing all zee public tenders. All town maintenance. Roofing. Drains. Plumbing." He waved a youthful hand to encompass the sheer volume of tasks affected. "Only things keep going vas on zee surfaces." He tapped the shining woodwork of the polished desks. "Inside public surfaces, gleaming. Outside, bright polished brass street lamps. Gas lighting is kept burning." He shrugged again. "But anyzing out of sight, vell he stopped paying. Many good citizens keep up labour, but...Time is a cruel mistress. Many vorkers forced to leave."

Ella swallowed, feeling physically sick. "Without wages they cannot afford to pay rent, I understand." She stood up, took several deep breaths, and paced the office. She knew that there was a strong community here, people who had lived for generations in Charmington. They would have bartered, traded, they would have taken care of each other, no one would have starved...

Hansel patted Ella's hand. "Zee craftsmans who made zee townships plumbing and ventilation systems vere second to none—zey built zee place to last."

Ella knew that years ago Sibylla had a falling out with town officials and forced out several of the leading craftsman families whose ancestors had designed the town's plumbing networks and connected the thermal seams and water. The public infrastructure must be under a great strain, and the gas system was much more modern. Installed under two decades ago when magic was banned and gas lighting was required to replace the magical fairy lights.

As if sensing her thought process, Hansel added, "I have sent Mr. Beau under zee town hall to assess basements, drains and plumbing. There vas a pipe bursting some months back."

"But Mr. Beau maintains the gas lamps," Ella said, flapping her hands, surprised by Hansel's choice. "Does he know *anything* about the town's plumbing systems?"

"Yes, some." Hansel tilted his head. "Beau's father apprenticed to plumbing craftsmans many years ago. And...zere is no one else left. Needs must."

Ella sighed. No one else left. Of course. Beggars could not be choosers. "Thank you, Hansel. I know you are doing your best with what little resources there are."

Hansel flipped open his pocket watch. "Any minute now, I am expecting Mr. Beau's final report. If you care to vait?"

Ella pacing again. She had heard about the broken pipe. Harold and Goldi had both mentioned it. Documents in storage were ruined. Well, that wasn't the end of the world. Indeed, here she was, standing in the warm and dry, comfortable building. Surely it couldn't be that bad...they'd simply start paying for maintenance again...

How would they pay the maintenance staff?

Ella stopped in mid pace and clamped a hand to her face. Struck with the horrifying notion that Harold himself must have concluded. They could not 'simply' start paying for maintenance. The *kingdom* was on the verge of financial ruin. They didn't have the money to pay staff.

Where would they get money from? Would they be forced to accept Prince John's land rental proposal and build his horrible prison in Wyld Kingdom?

Footsteps rising on the staircase that connected into the basement levels echoed and Ella turned to the sound. A waft of Iron Drake shoe polish hit her senses and Hansel introduced Mr. Beau, the shoeshine man and who was also in charge of the gas street lamps.

Ella held out her hand to him. "Mr. Beau, a pleasure."

"Mornin', your ladyship," Mr. Beau said, touching his forelock and sweeping his cap off and turning it about his hands. His reddened knuckles peaked out from patched fingerless gloves. He ducked his head. "If you'll excuse me, my hands are a bit grimy."

Ella quickly withdrew her hand, aware she had unintentionally embarrassed him. "Of course, and please accept my thanks for all your hard work." She had met Mr. Beau on several occasions and always found him helpful and capable.

But until this moment, she didn't realise that perhaps she owed him a debt of gratitude far greater than she knew. Had he been working, keeping their streets lit and safely maintained, without receiving payment for his labours?

"We are lucky to have you, Hansel tells me you are assessing the plumbing?"

Mr. Beau shuffled on the spot. "Ah well, as I says to Mr. Hansel. I'll take a look and help if I can. Me dad were the proper chap for it. I just know the basics. Loosie leftie and rightie tightie." He chuckled and Ella smiled blandly at whatever plumbing joke had just gone over her head, instead finding herself braced for whatever terrible news his inspection must surely have uncovered.

"Vell, Mr. Beau, vat is your assessment?" Hansel looked expectantly.

Mr. Beau smiled and knocked on the staircase balustrade. "Touch wood, the town hall and post office gas lines are in sound order. As for the plumbing, town hall side down to the river, from what I can see, the drains are not too bad. I still need to take a look at the upper east side substation. Can't access that from here."

Hansel nodded and took up a pencil to jot down some notes. "Good, good, I can arrange zee keys for zee substation."

Ella let out a breath, relief loosening the tension in her old bones. Magic preserve! Things might not be so dire after all!

But Mr. Beau's cap was still being turned around and around in his hands as he waited for Hansel to finish writing and signal he was ready for Beau to continue with his report.

When Hansel did, Mr. Beau's expression became anxious. "The gas line going south under the Playhouse nearby doesn't look good—Nigella had already been complaining that the stage lights weren't working—and now I know why. There's subsidence. That water damage you had me investigate. A partial collapse must have damaged the northern gas line." He hitched his thumb at the basement staircase. "I had to shut off their main gas valve here, and they will need to be told they can't use the building." He shuffled on the spot again. "That ain't the worst part. Gas could'a been pooling under the playhouse for months."

"Gas pooling?" Ella squinted, confused. "I always thought gas er, *floated* away?"

"Some kinds, yes, but the gas used for street lamps and such is heavier than air. Break in the line and it sinks. Acts much like water, ya see. Pools in the cracks and drains. Builds up, filling the voids like an underground lake."

"Oh dear. So there's a lake of gas pooled under the Playhouse? Is that a bad thing?"

Beau replied frankly, "Layman's terms, the playhouse is a death trap."

"Death trap..." Ella slowly repeated Mr. Beau's foreboding words. "The playhouse is a death trap..."

"Yes, *marm*, one spark and—*boom!*" Mr. Beau placed his cap squarely back on his head, expression grim. "Aye, and I can tell you the playhouse director Nigella Pickford is going to be more than a little upset. They'll have to find somewhere else to practise until the building foundations can be properly investigated and the plumbing lines repaired, and that won't be easy."

"Repaired?" Ella felt a sense of hope mixed with dread at her next question. "Can it be repaired?"

Mr. Beau shrugged. "Course! Beyond my abilities, mind, it will take a team of engineers, masons, builders and such."

Hansel waved his pencil. "Can you estimate the cost of the foundation and plumbing repairs?"

Mr. Beau sliced a hand empathically, *no*. "That's way above my basic knowledge. All I can say for sure is the repairs will be extensive and beyond my meagre know-how, and therefore expensive." He winked cheekily at Ella. "Still, that's what taxes are for, right? You'll have to get experts in, like, to assess the damage to the foundations.

The hot water leak that caused the subsidence must have been dripping away for years before the stonework sunk to damage the line. Don't know what you'll find when you start digging." He sucked in a fortifying breath. "Well, if you don't mind, I best give Nigella the bad news quick smart. She's over there right now, telling her theatre company about plans for the Christmas production."

Ella held up a finger. "Wait, Mr. Beau. I think it best I go with you when you speak to Nigella." She turned to exchange a tight glance with Hansel. "I am right in thinking we only have *bad news* for Nigella and her theatre company?"

Hansel tapped his own set of ledgers. "Correct. Zere is no money for repairs." He crossed his arms. "Hard times call for hard measures. Technically speaking, zee theatre is a luxury building, not a town necessity."

Ella's shoulders sagged. "I will do it. Inform Nigella. It is my responsibility in my role as director for rents and repairs to be the bearer of bad news." She gestured for Mr. Beau to go on ahead of her while she thanked Hansel for his work thus far on the financial reports.

"No more funding!" Mr. Beau blanched and straightened his cap when Ella caught up. "Cripes! I don't want to be the one to tell Nigella that! What's that expression them actors use—murder the messenger and all that?"

CHAPTER 4

THE PICKFORD PLAYERS' DEATH TRAP

THE PLAYHOUSE WAS A LARGE building located just beyond the town hall. It had been many years since Ella had set foot inside the theatre. But Mr. Beau knew the way, taking the back route through the town hall along corridors that she was unfamiliar with. They crossed the street and entered the back of the theatre to proceed through a warren of narrow corridors. As if to bolster her spirits, or perhaps just to provide polite conversation, Mr. Beau pointed out items of interest as he guided her through an area with ropes hanging like a shipyard, and large 'flats' of painted scenery from past productions.

"You appear well acquainted with the theatre," Ella said, gripping her walking stick, as he held a side door open and waited for her as they entered the back of the main stage.

"Oh, yes," Mr. Beau replied, "I usually do the stage lighting for Nigella, not to mention the heating, on account of the gas it uses. There she is now."

The light in the theatre was dim, but sunlight was filtering through from somewhere up high to illuminate the large wooden stage where Nigella and her cast had gathered.

On the front of the stage, Nigella Pickford, manager and owner of the company of 'Pickford Players', was also leaning on a walking stick, and Ella was reminded the actress had broken a leg a month or two back. Surrounding Nigella was a half-circle of actors, a few of whom Ella recognised. There was Spalding, grandson of the former mayor, and a gentleman called Bob, and his granddaughter Fishstix—whose true name was Felicity, but as a child she could not pronounce that, and so Fishstix had stuck. Ella had met Bob and Fishstix last month when she had mistaken the pair for actual castle guards. They had been dressed in uniform and practising marching, and she had commanded them to arrest a suspicious fellow. It was all rather embarrassing...

Beside Nigella was another familiar figure, the stout form of Mistress Fairweather, the indomitable matron of the Baker Street

Orphanage. Though usually dressed in practical and sturdy garments, today the matron was dressed in a multilayered muslin dress with white ribbons and frills, and topping off her elaborate outfit was a white bonnet festooned with ostrich feathers. The matron scooped up a matching feather fan that was resting atop a crate of green bottles off to the side of the stage and waved the feather fan towards a small group of children in the darkened front row.

Surely they were some of the matron's orphans. Normally they would have been wearing homely blue and yellow jerseys, but today were likewise dressed in matching white muslin outfits. All manner of frills spilling out their high-necked dresses, and white cashmere shawls clasped tightly across their shoulders. No doubt for all their lacy finery they were cold. The theatre was a large space and there appeared to be no heating.

Whatever Nigella had been saying to the actors, she cut off on spying Mr. Beau and Ella approach and the actress thumped her walking stick sharply beside one of a row of brass shell-shaped stage lights that ran the length of the front of the stage. "Beau! There you are! It's freezing in here." Her breath puffed in a cloud of steam. "None of the house lights or gas heaters are working! Is this any way to welcome our new sponsor?"

"About that..." Mr. Beau said, holding up hands to placate the glowering playhouse director as everyone's heads turned their way. "Lady Ella needs a word..." Bob and Fishstix, grinning at Ella, marched around and behind her, falling in, like two guards. They saluted and stamped heels to the stage boards. Ella managed a thin smile at their antics, hoping she wouldn't flush scarlet with embarrassment.

Nigella waved a hand magnanimously. "Her ladyship is always welcome..." She grinned wide and obsequiously to the lace-bedecked matron, Mistress Fairweather, beside her. "...as indeed are all *true* patrons of the arts. But before her ladyship speaks, first, I'm sure you're all *dying* to announce our most *pressing* and *important* matter—the play selected for the Christmas production. I have already introduced everyone to our new leading lady, Mistress Fairweather, who will stand in for me whilst I gain full mobility."

Ella caught a strained expression from Bob and an eye roll from Felicity, which she interpreted to mean, *There they go again! We'll be here all day at this rate!*

Nigella and Fairweather bowed to each other in an elaborate fashion of mutual subservience while the matron fluttered her fan and Nigella bent an awkward curtsey, hobbling back on her stick and gestured graciously to the crate of green bottles labelled *Lily's Health Tonic*. "Our thanks once again to Mistress Fairweather and her soon-to-be world-famous tonic, for sponsoring this year's Christmas production..."

Fan fluttering and curtseying interlude seemingly finished, Nigella drew breath, and projected her clear stage voice to those gathered, "Now, on to what our Christmas production will be this year. After much thought, I have decided we shall put on the Scottish play, *Lady MacDeath*."

"MacDeath?" The Pickford players gasped in horror. "You can't be serious! Lady MacDeath? The *cursed* play!"

The actors' troop shared confused looks with one another, as if they might have heard wrong, and even Ella was taken aback. Though she did not believe in *that* type of curse, she remembered all too well what had happened the last time the play had been performed in Charmington sixty years ago. Tragedy had befallen the cast and several people had died in very bizarre and nasty ways, including being burned alive and drowning.

Spalding, the former mayor's grandson, who had been limbering up on stage by stretching, spoke up, "Three people died in *Lady MacDeath's* opening season! Everyone knows the only way to break the curse is '*three must die again*' before opening night. Otherwise disasters will befall the playhouse."

This elicited a bunch of head nodding and agreement from all but Mr. Beau, who was standing at the back covertly sniffing the air as if seeking gas leaks. He shook his head and tutted. "Four—not three. *Four* must die to break the playhouse curse because four died last time. Trampled, hanged, drowned and burned alive. Easy to remember, see..." Mr. Beau gestured, his knuckles peeking out the worn gloves as he thrust a thumb downward then up. "Knocked *down*, strung *up*." He repeated the thumbs down, thumbs up gesture. "Wet *down*, burned *up*."

Ella bit her bottom lip. A jolt of memory hit. She had seen children doing that very thing years ago, making a skipping rhyme from the tragic turn of events as they played...

...One, Two. If I am trampled, who shall hang?
Three, four, breathe no more.
Water in your lungs is better than five.
All the leading ladies burned alive!

Actually. Come to think of it, hadn't one of the victims been a Beau? Yes, the one who drowned... No wonder Mr. Beau was aware of the rhyme. He had probably been taunted with it as a child...

"Was it fire after water?" muttered Nigella, rubbing her chin. She turned to Ella as if seeking her opinion. "I recall the leading lady burned alive *before* their patron drowned? Fell down, burned up, hung up, wet and drowned?" Nigella suddenly waved her hands as if that wasn't the point. "It's a *ridiculous* superstition, but I respect your decision not to audition, Spalding. Fortunately, I have offered the lead male role to Claude."

"Wait, what?" Spalding cried, the young man's tone enraged. "But *Claude's* not a member of the troop! He owns a bookshop!" Spalding turned to beseech his fellow actors. "That goes against the terms of our company's agreement! I have first rights on male lead!"

Ella rocked back on her feet, observing Spalding's swift reversal of objections. Despite initial resistance to the cursed play, he clearly wanted the leading role. How quickly opinions were reversed when fortunes were threatened...

She caught Nigella and Fairweather exchanging knowing smiles. Indeed, something was afoot here... Mistress Fairweather blushed and covered her face shyly with the ostrich feather fan. Ella frowned. Hmm, perhaps Fairweather, as their sponsor, had put that suggestion to Nigella? Claude was very handsome, and a former actor of some repute, having moved to Charmington township from the city of Avalon not long ago...

Nigella pulled a square of card from her pocket and squinted at it before continuing, "Right, before our new leading lady tells us about her...*simply delicious and nutritious tonic, filled with a patented blend of seven essential ingredients required to sustain a life of health* ..." Nigella waved a hand to Fairweather and her green box of bottles labelled *Lily's Health Tonic*. "Lady Ella has a few words she wanted to say..."

Ella had almost forgotten her purpose for being there, so caught up in the human drama that her heart leapt into her throat when Nigella suddenly spoke her name. Oh dear...

Hold your head high, old girl, she told herself before taking a deep breath and saying firmly, "Due to circumstances beyond the control of the Charmington council, I personally regret to inform you all that there is no more funding available. Furthermore, due to the playhouse building's bad state of repair—to the point it's dangerous—the theatre will be shut down. Effective immediately. Everyone, please leave the building."

From the sea of horrified faces, Mr. Beau tilted his head and gave her a wink. "Could it be that the curse of *Lady MacDeath* has just begun?"

CHAPTER 5

KNOCKED DOWN

"WHAT? What?" Mistress Fairweather uttered in shock and outrage. Each 'what' increasing in volume and pitch and she flung her ostrich feather fan to the floorboards. "But this is my debut! The launching of my career!" Her face reddened beneath her overtly powdered cheeks and she clenched her large hands into angry fists. "You can't do this! I pay my taxes!"

"This is a matter of public safety," Ella said and turned on her heel. The first rule of governing was, *you can't reason with a mob*, and she had no intention of standing on this stage, arguing a minute longer than necessary.

If she moved, people would follow. Then, once they were all safely outside, they could vent their anger and frustration rather than remain standing around on a potential tinder box above the lake of gas Mr. Beau had discovered.

With a shrug, Bob and Fishstix fell in step behind Ella, not breaking character from their self-chosen acting role of spear carriers. Their marching movement, along with the additional assistance of Mr. Beau gently corralling the confused company of actors, "Move along, move along," while waving his arms like he was shooing a flock of sheep, got the crowd moving towards the exit. "Let's all calmly flee the death trap, shall we?" Mr. Beau added cheekily. "Before we spark the pooling gas and things turn crispy?"

Someone was enjoying themselves, Ella thought sourly.

"Children, children," Nigella called gently, ushering the small audience of Fairweather's orphans to her, "come, come, at once."

"Quickly!" Mistress Fairweather added, with a foot stomp, and pointing to her bottled merchandise. "Collect the tonics. Leave none behind."

Ella made it out onto the front steps ahead of the meandering actors who were peppering Nigella with questions, or idly gossiping about the future of the company without a playhouse in which to perform.

"Once I performed *Joan of Arc* in a barn," Nigella said, and she flourished her hand, "without a roof, in the rain!"

"Not a dry eye in the place, I bet," Mr. Beau quipped before ducking out of the way as the orphanage matron caught up to Nigella by pushing her way past Spalding and through a bunch of actors carrying fake swords.

"But this is *my* acting debut!" Fairweather repeated, clutching three tonic bottles to her bosom while somehow juggling her fan, a parasol, and also towing a child in her ostentatious wake. "You promised everything would be perfect! I didn't *pay* for the privilege of a barn! Roofless or otherwise!"

"The show will go on," Nigella said pragmatically, but determined, as the players emptied on the street, "nothing can stop the arts!"

One of the other actors milling about whispered, "Not even curses?" aside to Spalding, who had his arms crossed and was kicking at the snow on the steps outside the theatre.

Ella looked for a suitable place to stop and address everyone that was far enough away from the playhouse but not out on the road in between the playhouse and the town hall, which was bustling as carriages drew up to a gathering crowd. It appeared a rally for one of the mayoral candidates was about to take place. Many townsfolk were holding aloft freshly painted banners with slogans that read, '*The numbers don't lie*' and '*Marley adds up!*'

Ella sighed. Perhaps this wasn't the best place to stand and answer the actors' questions. She didn't want to have to yell over the political rally crowd to be heard.

Then again, maybe she should ask if her friend Sally would allow everyone into her haberdashery and millinery business at the top of the square? She knew that Nigella was also a close friend with the elderly milliner, and quite likely Fairweather had commissioned her outlandish ostrich feather hat from Sally. Actually, come to think of it, Sally was finalising her adoption of her ward Olly this month. She probably wouldn't appreciate an aggravated Fairweather associating her shop with the demise of her burgeoning acting career. No, Ella would just have to speak to everyone out here on the playhouse steps...

But before Ella could utter a word, a middle-aged man dressed very finely with a red silk cravat, smart double-breasted black woollen coat, cane and top hat, rushed up, bellowing, "Charles Spalding! Son, what are you doing here?"

The man, Bertram Spalding, Ella realised on recognising the recently deceased mayor's middle-aged son, and now favoured candidate to be the next duly elected mayor, continued shouting, "We agreed you would quit this acting nonsense and help with my campaign!" And with a lower tone, Bertram growled, jabbing his cane at the people alighting from carriages over at the growing rally across the street. "That penny-pinching bookkeeper upstart, Jacob Marley, is stealing my votes!"

Spalding pushed off from his slouched lean against the stone column. "No, Father. You and mother agreed on my behalf!" He grabbed a prop sword from a fellow actor and raised it aloft, and then, like a call to arms, shouted, "Acting is my life! My true family! We few, we happy few! This bold troupe of men and women I call my brothers."

His fellow troupe members, those still clutching their array of prop weaponry, suddenly raised their swords at Spalding's back, and cheered in unison, "Huzzah!" like an elite military squad.

"Acting is my life!" Spalding shouted again, caught up in the moment of drama and raised his fist at his finely dressed father. "I will never cease! Never quit! I shall act in *Lady MacDeath* on Christmas Day!"

"Huzzah! Huzzah!" cheered the Pickford Players, thrusting sword tips in the air with each resolute cry. "MacDeath! MacDeath!"

But Bertram was no longer paying attention to his son's theatrics. "Odious, working class piece of trash!" he growled under his breath while casting a disparaging look at his political rival Marley who had just stepped down from a carriage across the street to his own cheering crowd of onlookers. Clutching his cane tightly, Spalding's father's glum expression suddenly turned assertive, and he pointed at the faux swordsmen surrounding his son. "I'll pay every man-Jack-of-you, a silver coin, to come stand alongside me and join my rally right now!"

"Huzzah!" cried the actors, immediately switching loyalty from their fellow actor to follow an *actual* next meal ticket, and they rattled their sabres and cried *huzzah* some more.

The actors' hungry fervour caught the attention of the opponent's rally across the street and Jacob Marley himself called out, "The numbers are against you, Bertie old chap! Give up while you're behind! *Haha!*" And his supporters all laughed along and hoisted their slogan banners higher and chanted, "The numbers don't lie! Accountability matters! Marley for mayor! Marley for mayor!"

Seemingly enraged, eyes fixed on his political foe, and with a newly minted 'army' of actors at his back, Spalding's father Bertram tugged at his red cravat, flung one last a look of utter betrayal at his wayward son and growled, "You'll be an actor over my dead body!"

Bertram stepped off the curb and marched across the road with his sword-waving entourage a step behind. The two political groups clashed, shouting insults and waving fists or banners. A horse reared, spooked by the ruckus. It bolted. Bertram jumped back, gasping. Straight into the path of a horse-drawn carriage.

Bertram was knocked to the cobbles. Horses' hooves and wheels obscured Ella's view. Women screamed and somewhere in Ella's memory, she heard children singing,

> *...One. Two. If I am trampled, who shall hang?*
> *Three, four, breathe no more.*
> *Water in your lungs is better than five.*
> *All the leading ladies, burned alive!*

◄━●━•━•━━

A SECOND AGO, ELLA HAD seen Bertram in the middle of the road, having jumped clear of the spooked horse. He was gasping.

Suddenly, another horse and carriage obscured her view. A scream rang out, and Bertram was on the ground. There was an alarmed outcry and people rushing to his side.

"Magic preserve! Is he hurt?" Marley, Fairweather, and others coming to Bertram's aid hid Ella's view of the toppled man. Had a carriage wheel or a hoof had struck him? She hadn't seen. "What a terrible accident!"

Bertram's son, Spalding, stood nearby, mouth hung agape in abject horror at his father lying prone on the cobbles. "Accident? That was no accident!" the actor cried, his voice pitched high with terror as he dropped his faux sword and clutched his temples. "It's the curse! *Three must die* before opening night! It's started!" And with a tormented wail, he turned away and fled back into the dark confines of the condemned playhouse.

"Four—not three! Four must die to break the playhouse curse!" Mr. Beau corrected at Ella's side, before striding past her and the unusually dumbstruck Nigella, and joined the crowd surrounding the fallen Bertram.

Ella inched forward with the aid of her stick, crossed the frosty cobbles to witness Marley, Fairweather, and Mr. Beau, all fussing with Bertram's red cravat. Marley, in near hysterics, had his hands clutched about Bertram's throat, shaking the man and shouting, "You awful old codfish! Don't you dare die on me!"

Fairweather slapped Marley's hands away. "Loosen his tie, idiot!" Bodily she elbowed the accountant aside.

Mr. Beau stood over, tutting. "Think you're wasting your time, Mistress, to be fair."

Marley snapped at the maintenance man, "I won't win like this! I won't!" He snatched Beau's coat lapels, his eyes wide, and shook the smaller man.

"Lady Luck has struck down your only serious contender, Marley," Beau quipped, and yanked his coat collar from Marley's grasp. "The mayoral race went from a two horse race to one..."

Marley drew back. "Don't be so cheap and vulgar." He stood up and shouted, "Where's the doctor? Someone fetch Doctor Hyde!"

"Struck down?" Nigella was mumbling beside Ella, apparently in shock. "The poor man was choking—didn't you see him gasping?"

"I'm sure he's still breathing!" Fairweather pressed an ear to Bertram's face. "We must administer a dose of my patented tonic! Marley, you know it works wonders!"

"Beau is correct, we are too late..." Marley's nose wrinkled, and he pulled her away even as she uncapped a green bottle. "Even your marvellous tonic, Mistress, can't bring back the dead."

Ella stood back, making room as some fellows with stretchers were allowed through to the stricken man.

As people bundled Bertram's body away, Marley picked up the fallen top hat of his political rival. A strange look of disgust and yet satisfaction crossed his face. He caught Ella observing him and dusted the hat off before turning away.

"Someone should go after Spalding," Ella said quietly to Nigella, touching the theatre woman's arm. But she, like Ella, was impeded by her bad leg.

"Go back into the *death trap* of a theatre?" Bob said at Ella's back, echoing a strained look with his granddaughter Fishstix. "When there's a *curse* at large! That is what I heard you say, Beau. Death trap?"

Beau rolled his eyes. "Actors!" he grumbled, adjusting his cap and then slapping Bob on the shoulder. "Fine, I'll go. I know that place like the back of my hand. But someone better come looking for me if I'm not there at supper."

If I am trampled, who shall hang?

Unbidden, the lines echoed in Ella's mind. She gave herself a sharp mental shake. Nonsense. There was no curse. Bertram's death was a tragic accident, not the beginning of a curse... No one was about to be hanged.

CHAPTER 6

THE GOOSE CHASE

DRAWING HER THOUGHTS TOGETHER, ELLA realised all the actors attentions had been directed away from her announcement that the theatre must be shutdown, and Bertram's untimely death had given her the perfect opportunity to "Exit stage right" as actors said, and resume the main task for her day—helping young Tom figure out how to return to his original human form.

Taking her leave, she made her apology to Nigella, then nodded to Bob and Fishstix, her self-appointed guards and snapped a commanding, "Dis—*missed!*" To which they saluted crisply, before breaking character and strolling off somewhere.

Ella clutched the silver head of her walking stick and hobbled off around the side of the town hall, heading back into Northgate Square and Sally's haberdashery, where she assumed young Tomcat must be waiting.

She tapped her stick on the cobblestones when a child near Sheriff Axel's police station caught her attention. The child, dressed in a very fine outfit of dark blue velvet britches and matching cutaway jacket, appeared entirely engaged in shaping snow drifts into lumpy snowmen. However, Ella spied the child, not once, but twice, halting from their industry to enter an animated conversation with one of the influx of strangers dressed as hunters who squinted at the posters tacked to the police noticeboard. Much hand waving and pointing followed, as if the child was giving directions to the hunter. Each occasion, the verbal exchange finished with the newcomer doffing their cap and then set off at a brisk pace. A smug grin flashed on the child's face as they watched the hunter walk away across the square.

Ella narrowed her eyes. Something was up there. What was the boy up to? Suddenly, the child saw they were being studied, and their grin widened. The child trotted over and Ella realised with a jolt of surprise it was Sandy, one of the Baker Street orphanage boys, who she was far more accustomed to seeing dressed in homely blue and yellow knitted jumper and corduroy trousers, and more often than not in the company of their little sister Sam, who had a clever pet rat.

"Good morning, Sandy," Ella greeted as the orphan skipped over. "I almost didn't recognise you."

"I know, right?" Sandy chuckled, posing to show off his smart little outfit. "I look like a right toff, don't I? Me and Sam is being adopted by Mistress Fairweather herself!"

Ella blinked, a little surprised but all the same, glad to hear the news. "That is wonderful. I am very pleased for you both."

"Thanks, but actually I wanted to ask. Have you seen Sheriff Axel's poster?" Sandy said quietly, tugging Ella's sleeve and his cheerful expression turned worried. "Come, read this!"

Following the young orphan, Ella walked up to the noticeboard outside the police station and read the poster with horror.

> **Reward. *Fifty gold coins to anyone catching***
> ***a LIVE talking cat.***

"Magic preserve!" Ella gulped, suddenly looking here and there in case Tomcat was walking across the square toward them from the haberdashery at that very moment. Her earlier guess about the strangers' purpose was correct! They *were* hunting Tom!

On seeing her agitation, young Sandy said, "Me and Sam has been giving people false directions and stuff all morning." He pointed west. "I sends them to the animal sanctuary on Hot Cockle Lane."

"But there isn't an animal sanctuary on Hot Cockle Lane any more?" Ella voiced, momentarily confused. "Doctor Hyde's hospital is in that old warehouse building beside the river now."

"I know." Sandy gloated, polishing his knuckles on the velvet lapel of his jacket. "See, Sam is hanging around outside the hospital and she tells them what they really need to do is go ask at the Huntsman tavern in Southgate..."

Ella tilted her head. Hansel and Gretel, currently busy at the post office, owned the Huntsman tavern.

"... only when they gets there, they either finds the tavern is closed, or they bump into the Chelton butchers across the street. If they do, Mrs. Chelton is telling them she just saw a man dressed in black talking to a cat, and they were heading out the gate and discussing their journey to Nottingham via the ice road."

"So you're sending them on a merry goose chase all over town?" Ella nodded, a sense of relief and gratitude flooding her. Thank goodness for all her and Tom's good friends. She squeezed Sandy's shoulder. "Thank you, Sandy."

Sandy ducked his head and blushed. "It were Miss Cassidy's idea."

He was about to say more when the door to the police station opened and the Sheriff kicked a cat-shaped snowman off the station's steps. "Stop leaving these here!" Axel roared at Sandy. He tugged up the collar of his heavy black coat and stormed over.

Sandy scurried off, giving Ella one last wave and a conspiratorial grin.

Ella stepped in front of Axel's tall, brooding figure, afraid he might chase after the boy, but Axel's focus was only on inspecting the talking-cat reward poster, as if expecting to find it damaged or altered.

"*Humph*," Axel muttered, running a hand through his dark hair, on seeing the poster was intact. A folded copy of the Nottingham newspaper tucked was under his arm and he unfurled it and tapped a small advert placed in the classifieds. "You might as well give up and turn that cat over," he told Ella. "Amateurs will waste their time chasing the brats' false leads, but the professional hunters won't. And it's just a matter of time before the streets are filled with them." He touched his forelock in mimicry. "Your ladyship." And dropped the newspaper at Ella's feet before heading back inside the station.

Odious, contemptible man! Ella thought to herself.

And to think that Sheriff Axel still did not know that Tom April, the rookie guardsman who had served under Axel, *was* the mysterious talking cat he searched for! It was almost amusing. Almost, but not quite. Tomcat's freedom was at stake, after all. What would the sheriff do if he ever caught the cat he hunted?

By leaning heavily on her walking stick, and with a wince, she bent to pick up the paper, which she discovered was a week old. The advert wording was similar to the poster.

> **Fifty gold coins to capture the**
> **Charmington Talking cat ALIVE.**
> **Deliver to Sheriff Axel.**

Ella swallowed. Oh dear. By advertising in this newspaper, Axel had broadcast the reward across two kingdoms—Wyld Kingdom and Sherwood! And many more might read the paper...

Goodness. Fifty gold coins was a lot of money! A year's wages to many. Where could he have even gotten his hands on such a sum...?

Hollow dread filled Ella's veins like ice as the realisation struck home.

Axel *didn't* have the money. He didn't need it. Axel just wanted the cat captured. He wouldn't care if the hunters were paid or not.

And regardless of if the sheriff had any intention of making a payout, the influx of strangers in town that morning suggested the sheriff's advert was working.

Which meant that the longer Tom April remained stuck as Tomcat, the higher the likelihood one of these hunter types could capture and turn him over to Axel. Tom was in real danger.

Ella's plan today to figure out how to restore Tom to his human body was now nothing short of imperative.

Chapter 7

The Golden Goose

WITH AS MUCH DIGNITY AS she could muster, well aware he was probably watching her expression from the window, Ella carefully folded Axel's newspaper, tucking it under her arm. "Littering is beneath me," she muttered to herself, partly to quell her urge to tear the Reward poster off from the noticeboard, but that would only prove to Axel he had gotten under her skin. No, the answer was to appear entirely unaffected...

Remain calm, remain calm, she told herself.

Seething internally, Ella turned on her heel and ventured past the frozen-over unicorn water fountain statue as if to stride down Mercer Lane, but once there were people behind her, masking her direction, Ella turned at the bank corner and ducked down the alley off beside the abandoned Cluckoo shop, to the back entrance of Sally's haberdashery where she hoped Tomcat was safely holed up.

Ella knocked on the wooden backdoor to Sally's business and residence and waited as she mulled over Axel's timely reminder of her initial goal for the day, to find out how to switch Tom back into his human form.

She glanced at the date of the newspaper Axel had dropped. A week old. And the classified advert was *small*. Good. Hopefully, it wouldn't be likely to attract too many fortune hunters other than the handful of strangers already wandering around town.

Then again, potentially *anyone* could be lured by Axel's advert for several weeks to come—the newspaper had a good distribution. Any stranger might be a "fortune hunter" even those not dressed in typical hunting gear. After all, catching a cat was theoretically something *anyone* could do... Dear, oh dear, this was a worrying development, she and Tom would have to progress with the utmost caution...

"Sorry to keep you waiting, Your Highness," Sally said, opening the door at last. The elderly milliner appeared a little flustered. She wore a white apron over her polka dot gown, and several feathers clung to her hair. But despite her unkempt appearance, Sally had a rather large grin, which she kept trying to suppress. "Olly has a new pet bird—

ahem—and I didn't want it to escape..." Sally smirked, bit her lips, and gestured for Ella to go through to the backroom of the haberdashery.

Ella inhaled the familiar fragrance of lavender that habitually hung around the bolts of silk and hat forms in the back of Sally's shop and she sought for signs of this new pet, expecting to see a bird cage or hear the chirp of a songbird. Ella drew up short. Upon the large cutting table sat a white goose nestled in a colourful paisley-patterned shawl.

"A goose?" Ella blinked at young Olly, who, resplendent in their customary yellow velvet, was leaning on the far end of the broad table and twirling a ribbon in their hand.

"A *golden* goose," the child said most solemnly, but avoided eye contact.

Ella squinted. Young Olly had a penchant for all things golden, but surely she must have misheard the former orphan. "Is that a suitable pet? A goose, I mean. Aren't they rather aggressive?"

As if offended, the goose head swivelled, beady eyes fixedly cast a dark gaze her way as Ella scanned the floor under the table where Tomcat must be hiding, keeping out of the way. "Where is Tom? Gracious, tell me he isn't actually wandering around outside, is he?"

"He was here a second ago," Sally said, stifling a giggle.

The large goose moved again. The head tipped forward and then fell off its body.

Ella flinched back, confused, staring at the white goose head on the floor. "Magic preserve! What's going on here?"

Olly burst out with laughter. Ella suddenly made sense of what she was seeing as a cat's head stretched up from the paisley shawl wrapped around the goose's—around Tomcat's body. "Tom?"

Olly swooped and picked up the goose head. "It's a hat, see! A goose head hat disguise!"

Ella gently took the offered object and turned it over in her hands. Every detail was meticulously crafted. "My goodness, it's very lifelike! I really thought I was seeing a goose, especially when it—er, Tom—moved." She gave herself a mental shake and handed the goose head disguise back to Sally.

"It's nearly finished. I just need to add a chin strap so it stays securely in place." Sally gestured to the shawl wrapping around where Tom sat nestled. "Though we haven't quite figured out the legs either."

"I think wrapping my body with the scarf is fine," Tomcat said. "As long as Ella doesn't mind having to carry me, people won't even look at the rest of the body. I fooled you, didn't I?"

Ella nodded. "Most certainly! My goodness, this is a testament to your skill, Sally."

The older lady bobbed her head and placed a hand on her young ward's shoulders. "It was Olly's idea—you see, I have to make a golden goose for Nigella's Christmas production of *Jack and the Beanstalk*." She placed a hand to her lips, as if she'd spilled a secret. "Oh, Nigella hasn't announced the Christmas play yet, has she?"

Ella frowned. *Golden goose? Jack and Beanstalk? But Nigella had said she was putting on Lady MacDeath. Or rather, no, there would not be a play at all.* "I hope Nigella paid you upfront," Ella said with a sigh, looking around at the cutting room where there were several goose head prototypes on the shelves and feathers littering the floor. Sally must have put a lot of time and effort into constructing the goose head.

"Yes, yes," Sally said, distractedly, avoiding Ella's gaze, and gave Olly a broom. The child swept up the feathers Tomcat shook loose as he stretched and shook himself free of the shawl. "Excuse the mess, it's the one downside. The feathers get everywhere."

"That might not be something you have to worry about much longer. I'm afraid I had to shut the theatre down this morning..."

And while Sally made cups of fragrant honey-bark tea, Ella relayed the ghastly incidents of the morning starting from when Hansel gave her the dreadful news about the post office finances.

"Harold *wasn't* stealing money?" Sally stirred another spoon of sugar into the china teacup. "That is good news, I suppose?"

"Certainly," Ella replied, taking a sip of tea. "It could have been worse."

"And the playhouse building was filling up with gas?" Tomcat said, whiskers quivering. "What good fortune Mr. Beau discovered that and shut off the values or whatever in time."

Sally nodded, placing her silver spoon on a plate. "To think, if Harold's daughter hadn't been caught up in that counterfeiting business, Lady Ella, you would never have had Hansel check the post office accounts!" She turned to her young ward as Olly snapped a biscuit in half and held it out for Tomcat to share. "And then Hansel wouldn't have looked into the tenders that Harold managed, which in turn, Mr. Beau wouldn't have been asked to assess the state of the plumbing and gas maintenance."

Ella brushed her skirts across her lap, watching Tom gnaw on the biscuit, dropping crumbs everywhere. "Indeed, the silver lining to the cloud that was Harold Harper."

Sally folded her arms. "He's running for mayor, did you know?"

"What? No!" Ella responded, further appalled when Olly fanned out a handful of brochures that must have arrived with their post. They held one up with a picture of Harold's face plastered across it and a slogan that read: *Tradition! Tradition! Tradition!*

"The nerve of that man running for mayor! What if he wins?"

"I shouldn't worry," Sally offered consolingly. "Everyone else says the former mayor's son, Bertram, will be the next mayor."

On hearing Bertram's name, Ella's mind flash-backed to the past hour, the poor man standing, gasping in horror, in the middle of the carriageway a second before he was struck down. Why didn't he move out of the way? He must have panicked. Not able to throw himself clear. "It won't be Bertram, he was killed in a tragic accident this morning."

Sally blinked. "Oh, well...I suppose that opens the race up. I wonder who will take the lead now... perhaps his rival Marley? Though I fully intend to vote for the bookshop owner, Claude. He is very handsome. It would be nice to have a handsome mayor, don't you think?"

Ella reached for her walking stick propped up against the table and rose to her feet. There was nothing she could do for Bertram, but Tomcat was another matter, and still her most pressing responsibility. "Thank you for the tea, and for your kindness in constructing such a clever disguise to keep Tom safe. Tom and I must hasten over to Goldi's now. We're on a mission to see if she can aid us in restoring Tom."

"What do you look like as a human?" Olly said, curiously, leaning forward. "Are you short or tall?"

Tomcat shrugged. "Quite tall. The cook at my orphanage—Master Spicer—used to joke that I had Prince John's nose." He blinked up at Ella. "When we first met, you said I looked like someone you knew, right? King Arnold or Arthur, who lived a long time ago."

Ella thought back to the moment she had first seen Tom April, the newest member recruited to the castle guards. She thought she had seen a ghost. Tom April looked like King Arthur from the neighbouring kingdom of Avalon. She pushed the thought aside. She must have been mistaken. Arthur had died over fifty years ago. He hadn't been around twenty years ago to sire and then abandon a child Tom's age. "And as I recall, you said I must be extremely old!"

Olly laughed as Tomcat hunched with embarrassment. "You didn't know you were talking to a proper toff!"

Ella glanced at the goose head disguise on the tabletop. "Um...? How do I put it on Tom?"

"It's not quite done—I just need to adjust the strap so it will stay on securely," Sally said, fiddling with the item in question. "But if you need to go, I have a trolley basket that I use to carry my shopping. You can use that in the meantime. It's made from cane, so though it might be a bit snug within, I am sure Tom will be able to breathe quite comfortably. If you don't mind wheeling it along behind you, that is?"

She looked up inquiringly, and when Ella nodded, Sally said, "Olly, can you please fetch the basket? Thank you."

Olly went to fetch the trolley and Sally said, "I will have the goose hat disguise finished as soon as I can."

Ella agreed. The day was looking up! If only Tom could be convinced to stay hidden within the basket, his chances of being caught by one of Axel's fortune hunters were slim indeed. There really was very little to worry about.

CHAPTER 8

GOLDILOCKS AND THE QUICK FIX

DRAGGING THE WICKER TROLLEY BASKET behind her, and apologising in a whisper to Tom, who was nestled inside at every jolt, Ella mounted the steps to the front entrance of the terrace house, which Goldilocks had converted into her healing business, Magical Day Spa. A three-storey building in white-dressed stone, the row of houses was located on the edges of the upper East Side, Charmington's most desirable neighbourhood.

Ella had been here just a month ago. She had brought Tomcat to be cured and cleansed after he'd become ill from black magic contamination—and his lovely white fur had been all stained black from chimney soot. Goldi and her staff had done a wonderful job, cleansing and soaping his fur into pristine condition while scouring the black magic taint that had coated his front paw pads.

Today, the spa appeared closed for business again, now that the ban on magic was reinstated. However, although they had removed the signage, sounds of movement came from inside. Ella knocked on the door, which swung open. She could hear people mumbling further along and the clang of buckets being moved across the polished wooden floors in the back spa rooms. "Goldi? Are you there?" Ella called, venturing into the plush entrance hall and hefting the trolley awkwardly up the last step behind her.

Aware he was off the street, Tomcat's head popped up from the wicker lid and he sprung lightly out from the shopping basket onto the thick Persian carpet.

"We're down the back," Goldi's welcoming voice called, echoing on the ornate plaster ceilings and chandelier above.

Ella and Tom ventured further inside to where the voices heralded and peeped through the doorway into the sunlight-filled spa room. Two ladies on ladders were wiping the large picture windows, and Goldi was industriously polishing and waxing the leather furniture. No doubt a deep-clean before finally shutting the business down now. "I am sorry for interrupting," Ella said after quickly explaining she had come for an expert opinion on her lodger Tom's *special* condition. "I confess we only decided to act on this today. We can come back another time. I see you are busy with spring cleaning."

"You're here now, and it's time we had a break," Goldi said kindly, as if it was no trouble at all. Goldilocks was a tiny craftswoman. She wore overalls today, and had wrapped her pink bouffant hair in a striking lime-green scarf.

She set her lemon-polish scented cloth aside and signalled to the other women to go and take their lunch breaks. "Besides," Goldi intoned knowingly, "if the strangers wandering around town are anything to go by, the faster we help Tom, the safer he'll be. I saw Axel's reward poster for a talking cat outside the police station too." She patted a freshly polished white leather couch. "Jump up here on the assessment bench, Tom. I'll take a look at you." Goldi turned back to Ella. "And I'll give your knees a quick jolt of pain-fade magic too while you're here. I noticed you were limping."

"Yes! Do Ella's knees first! I keep telling her to take something for the pain and she never listens!" Tomcat said, and while Goldi prepped to attend to Ella, he did as he was bid, stretched out across the plush leather and blinked up at them both.

"Should I stand or sit?" Ella asked.

"Standing is fine," Goldi said distractedly, opening a drawer. "I know this spell, like the back of your knee!" She held up an amber wand. "Hold your breath now—one, two!" She tapped the toes of Ella's boots and a shimming-bubbly sensation zipped up Ella's legs.

"That is so much better!" Ella exclaimed as the pain dissolved. "Thank you!"

"My pleasure!" Goldi laughed, waving her amber wand like an orchestra conductor.

Tom's green cat eyes sparkled. "What were you saying before? There's a reward poster to capture me? So that's why Sally and Olly were so insistent on making the golden goose disguise."

"Yes, and there's also a classified advert in the *Nottingham Times*." Ella rolled over a second stool and sat herself down alongside Goldi's footstool. "You will need to be very cautious, Tom—the reward Axel is offering is equivalent to a year's wages. The lure of that much money could tempt many ordinary people in Charmington to catch a talking cat. Not that I believe Axel really has such an amount of gold lying around." She shook her head and sighed. "Hopefully, the sensible residents will also have come to the same conclusion and think the whole thing is a hoax—the idea of a talking cat is enough for anyone familiar with magic to dismiss the idea as absurd."

Goldi hummed thoughtfully to herself as she adjusted the fairy lights hanging above Tom on the examination couch. "That's an excellent point..." She squinted at Ella for a minute. "How exactly *did* you turn a person into a cat? I've always been curious... The amount of power required to perform such a spell is mind-boggling. Even talking as we are, witnessing it for myself, I still find the concept absurd."

"Technically, *I* didn't turn Tom into a cat," Ella responded, folding her hands in her lap.

"I did it myself!" Tomcat nodded, whiskers fanning as he relaxed on the leather recliner. "I wished on a star!"

"Oh, yes, the star thing," Goldi said. "I think you mentioned that. But, then, Ella, to actually *maintain* the spell. You would have to be *constantly* tapping directly into the wyld magic of the entire kingdom! How can you do that when Tomcat is freely roaming around?"

Ella tapped her walking stick on the floor to emphasise the point. "Quite so, but that's part of it, you see, Goldi. It's only Tom's *essence*— his *personality*—that is being hosted within the body of my little cat, Tilly. Tom's human body, Tom April himself, is safely housed within one of the pumpkins in my garden."

"Say that again?" Goldi blinked. "Wait—Tom here is Tom *April*? That new castle guardsman? The one who went missing? But Tom April was over six feet tall—a big strapping lad! And you're telling me his body is somewhere *in* a pumpkin?"

"It is quite a large pumpkin, mind," Ella added. "Tom's human body was gravely injured after the, er, *essence swap,* you see, and the pumpkins took it upon themselves to form a sort of cocoon around him, and keep him in stasis."

"Oh, so it's kind of an illusion, not really a full physical swap," Goldi rocked back on her footstool as if everything now made sense. "Tom's *human body* hasn't transformed at all. It's the personalities that have been swapped. Now I understand. Oh, yes, that wouldn't take so much magic—no doubt the pumpkins themselves are tapping into the wyld magic in the soil."

Ella and Tom both leaned forward. "Do you have any idea how to reverse it?"

CHAPTER 9

GOLDI'S RISK ASSESSMENT

GOLDI TIPPED HER HEAD. "One would assume that once the injured body heals, both cat and human essences should naturally return to their original, er, containers."

"Yes, that's what I concluded too," Ella agreed, feeling a little smug her magical diagnosis was the same as Goldi's.

"But it's taking so long!" Tom bemoaned, flicking his tail across the plush leather. "Five months already. And Cassidy is leaving town tomorrow on the dawn river barge." He sat up straight. "You're a healer, Goldi. We thought maybe you could speed up the healing? Help nudge the pumpkins along?"

"Remind me. What magical variety were you growing?" Goldi asked, fetching out a cloth facemask and a pair of white sparkly gloves from a nearby cabinet. "Some kind of fabricator species?"

"That's right," Ella said. "It was a strain I crossbred from a *constructor* specimen that are the backbone of most pumpkins transformed into carriages, with another form used in treehouses." Ella thought back on the years ago when she had lovingly cultivated the pumpkins. "Following several experiments, I gave them a big jolt of wand magic to transform and grow into the cottage."

"Ahh, clever. You combined a pumpkin variety known for transformation spells, and *super-sized* it to grow from a treehouse to a cottage. Smart." Goldi tied the cloth mask across her face and then reached over to the cabinet once again and exchanged the amber wand for one made of crystal.

"Ah, yes, *super-sized*, that's an apt description," Ella said fondly, thinking of her riverside cottage where she now lived. She had originally grown the cottage as a wedding gift for her younger sister, Cinderella, and her husband, Richard. Their happiness ended when disaster struck. Cinderella died, and her husband and young son, Sage, disappeared, never to be seen again.

Although that wasn't entirely true. Ella had learned recently that Richard wasn't who he had claimed. He wasn't a hard working wood-cutter; he was a prince, the elder brother in fact of Prince John, who was now the regent of the neighbouring kingdom of Sherwood. But the child...what had happened to Cinderella's and Richard's little boy Sage?

"Hey! Cassidy's colleague, Ace, had some magical rose-tinted glasses!" Tomcat said, sitting up. "When you look through them, you can *see* my essence glowing. Where did you put them, Ella? Maybe Goldi should take a look?"

Ella blushed and stared at her hands. "I'm afraid that rogue, Rooster, stole Ace's spectacles from me. Picked my pocket..."

"That's a shame," Tomcat said, folding his tail under his furry body.

Goldi waved the concern away. "It's all right. I understand the situation. Your human essence, your spirit, is connected to the cat's body via the pumpkins, who are a conduit for our kingdom's powerful Wyld magic, and they have become a cocoon for your human body." She waved the crystal wand in the air, looping it around, and then tapped the couch. "I will attempt to *force* the human essence in the cat via a magical dispersion push or jolt to dislodge it. In theory, I should be able to channel the conscience all the way back to the pumpkin patch. Provided the human body has healed, your spirit will leave the cat's body and snap right back into your proper head. Easy peasy."

"Then I'll...er, hatch?" Tomcat's ears dipped up and down as he stood up, eager to hear more.

"Basically," Goldi said. "It'll be a bit messy, but not disorientating. Assuming your body has fully healed, your natural reflexes should take over. Meaning, you'll instinctively know to break out through the pumpkin skin, even if your memories *aren't* intact, and you *don't* remember this conversation, or why you've woken up encased in a very large pumpkin."

"Wait, what? What do you mean, 'even if I don't remember this conversation'? Are you saying I might *lose* my memories? All the time I've spent as a cat..?" Tomcat's whiskers dipped. "All the conversations I've had with Cassidy over the past five months? Getting to know her? Her...getting to know me?" His shoulders slumped, rounder and rounder, and he curled up tightly on the couch. "I only arrived in Charmington for two weeks before I swapped bodies with Tilly. I barely knew Cassidy at all... And to be honest, I think she thought I was a bit of an oaf back then."

Ella exchanged a sympathetic look with Goldi, who placed a kindly hand on Tom's shoulder. "Chances are you'll keep all your precious memories, but it *is* a risk." She tugged the facemask down and looked up at Ella. "Come to think of it, I'm sure I read a book ages ago about memories and magical trauma. Someone had gone around gathering tragic tales of people who had swapped minds, or had their essences trapped in mirrors and things..." She tapped her toe as if thinking. "Do you know the book I mean? Maybe it was an article in an academic journal. Haversham used to subscribe to a bunch."

Ella shrugged. "It's not something I recall reading. But it is exactly the kind of thing we'd find in Haversham's private library—assuming it still exists. Tom and I can go and do some research. She had a very broad personal library and an extensive collection of academic journals on all kinds of magic. From basic domestic laundry spells, to grand matters of state espionage."

Goldi raised a finger. "Yes! That's a good point. Tell you what, you check the library at Haversham's, and I'll go check Sibylla's library at the castle." The little craftswoman looked thoughtful. "Though, if we can't find anything, you know you *could* always reach out to Merlin."

"If we must." Ella pulled a sour face. She'd had quite enough of her infamous brother with last month's dealings. If it wasn't for Merlin showing up, Cassidy wouldn't be moving to Avalon and Tom wouldn't have had to consider leaving or risk speeding up the restoration of his essence before the natural healing process was complete.

Not that she begrudged her friend Tom from wanting to carry on with his human life. He was a young man in love, after all. And it was *her* duty as a friend to help him have the opportunity to travel to Avalon.

An idea occurred. "The other option is Tom—in his current Tomcat form—seeks treatment in Avalon from one of the Royal Pendragon healing spas, but such a unique case, it would be costly..." Ella trailed off, reminded of the kingdom's dire financial state. They had very little money. She had donated her only valuable item, the flying carpet, which she had sold at an auction last month, to raise funds for the roof repairs of Doctor Hyde's charity hospital in Hot Cockle Lane.

"Then again," Goldi piped up, "you could approach the Fairy Council to rectify the situation."

"You could?" Tomcat's ears flicked up. "I'll tell them it was my fault because I wished on the star. They'd believe me, right?"

Ella flinched and folded her arms tightly. She'd prefer to go to Merlin for help rather than the council. They'd done her no favours!

Binding her magic on trumped-up charges of misuse of wishes, thanks to Haversham's meddling!

Goldi appeared to read Ella's body language because she added, "Forget I said that. We don't want to put you in more hot water if the council thinks you somehow got around their temporary banning of your magic. They'd make the punishment permanent and strip you of your magic forever!"

"No. I won't risk that!" Tom said loyally. "I'd stay as a cat for the rest of my life before risking that!"

Ella took a deep breath. Tom was a kind and noble young man. It was time she repaid his kindness, no matter the personal cost. "I'm sure it won't come to that. We'll do some research, see what we can find about the risks of you losing your memory once you return to your human form, Tom. Then you can decide if you want Goldi to snap your essence back into its proper body. Yes?"

Tomcat stamped his paws on the couch and saluted. "Agreed!"

"Just be careful when you visit Haversham's library..." Goldi muttered, opening the cabinet drawer again and extracting a new pair of white sparkly gloves from a stash of equipment. "Make sure you wear these bewitched protection gloves when handling the old books." The little lady glanced at Tomcat as she passed Ella the gloves. "Watch out for signs of black magic contamination—Tom is very sensitive, as you're aware, and any residue will make him quite sick."

Ella took the gloves. "Thank you, that's very kind."

"Just being practical," Goldi commented. "Haversham was a black magic user and I've treated a couple of accidental magic poisoning cases recently. Between me and you, I was thinking of paying a visit to Haversham's academy because it occurred to me that some people might have used last month's temporary magical amnesty to raid the abandoned school without understanding the risks."

Ella nodded. Black magic residue built up on items that were frequently handled. Typewriter keys. Coins. And old books, as Goldi acknowledged. And the effects were not always obvious, or the same. Some forms of black magic ingredients, such as unicorn blood, caused hallucinations, while other ingredients made people physically sick or worse, drove them mad. Black magic destroyed the fortunes of many who came into contact with it, and its usage was truly a curse, because over time the taint of black magic corrupted *all* minds, no matter how kind or noble they were to begin with.

Chapter 10

Apples and Lemons

TOM HOPPED BACK IN THE loaned trolley basket, and Goldi helped Ella lift it back down the steps to the cobblestone street out in front of the row of terrace houses. They parted ways, Goldi heading towards the castle, its snow-capped turrets looming in the distance, and Ella prepared the short distance along to where the street widened to the main broad avenue of East Avenue.

East Avenue was the heart of the upper East side, the wealthiest portion of the township, and the wide road was lined with wrought-iron lamps and benches, and dotted with winter-stripped cherry trees. "This is where I first meet Cassidy," came Tom's wistful voice from the basket interior, one of its wheels squeaking as Ella trekked the dampened stones.

"I know," Ella said, arranging the fold of her cloak to cover her chin and disguise the fact she was talking aloud to her shopping basket. She paused on the curb to cross the avenue when the familiar shimmer of silver bells and clip-clop of horses from behind heralded the approach of her sister Queen Sibylla's carriage. Ella ducked her head down, hoping the addition of Sally's basket made her silhouette less recognizable. If her twin was inside the ornate coach, hopefully she would pass by without stopping...

"Good afternoon, ma'am," called the coach driver from the box seat and Ella straightened, as if she hadn't been trying to hide from her sister as the carriage drew up alongside her and stopped. The two horses drawing the carriage stamped her hooves and shook their manes.

"And a good day to you as well, Dirk," Ella greeted, casting a surprised gaze at the new addition to the coachman's familiar silhouette—beside Dirk Turpin, was not only the now familiar sight of the white poodle, dressed in cute miniature tricorn hat, that mimicked the coachman, but also dressed in palace livery was the skinny lad called Cheapcuts, the only son of the butchers, Martha and Chelton.

The little poodle yipped, and Cheapcuts bobbed his head. "Aye, is that right? I will ask her ladyship," Cheapcuts said seriously to the small dog as it held up a paw. "Mr. Puddles wants to know why your cat is riding in that basket? He's worried it might have hurt his paw."

Dirk did a double take at the shopping basket as Tomcat pushed his head up and peered over the rim. "I'm fine, thanks for asking."

Cheapcuts' natural Wyld magical ability to communicate with animals was something Ella had learned recently when his mother, Martha, had confided in Ella a few months ago, worried what would become of the lad. A boy who could 'talk' to animals would not enjoy following in his father's footsteps and become a butcher...

"Cheapcuts is my new apprentice," Dirk said fondly, drawing the leather reins in close and passing them to the youth, a sure sign of his esteem and trust in the gangly lad. "He's mighty good with the horses—he's a regular *horse-picturer!*"

Mr. Puddles barked and the white horses both snorted and snuffled, puffing out great plumes of breath on the frosty air. Cheapcuts jangled the reins and clicked his tongue at the two horses in a soothing fashion as they tossed their heads.

Ella squinted at the boy. "What are they saying? Are they all right?"

"Horses tend to think in pictures not with words," Cheapcuts explained. "When they're happy, they picture carrots and apples. Unhappy, it's bitter or sharp things, like lemons and thorns."

"They refuse to drink from any of the mid-town water troughs," Dirk added. "Cheapcuts says they keep picturing fish."

"Hmm, the Hot Cockle Lane fishworks factory is probably in full production with the salmon run," Ella said. "It gets whiffy this time of year."

"Anyway, we need them in a good mood for when we take her majesty down to the mayoral candidacy speeches later on." The coachman jumped down from the box and adjusted something on the two horses' silver and black harness. "Better?"

"Aye, I'm getting apples again," Cheapcuts told the coachman.

"Apples it is! New harness must have been pinching." He clapped his hands in glee.

Ella by now had deduced that her sister Sibylla was *not* in the carriage, and she relaxed and watched the two men working so well together to calm the horses. Apprenticing Cheapcuts to Dirk was an excellent idea, and she wished she'd thought of it. "I rather wondered if Merlin might have offered you a scholarship to his school in Avalon, along with young Bethany?"

Cheapcuts shrugged, and shook off the notion like one who thought they would stay young forever, and opportunities would always be plentiful. "Awful long ways to go. Avalon's a big city, and me Da don't care much for the city. He spends more time out in Wyld woods than he does at home as it is. And me Ma, she'd never want to leave him." The boy wrapped the reins around one hand so he could doff his tricorn with the other, and he clasped it over his heart. "Up here I'm on top of the world."

"I am very pleased for the both of you, you'll make an exceptional team," Ella agreed, as Dirk stood back from his task with the horse bridle, his mature face creased with concern and while patting the necks of the twin carriage horses, he peered about, studying the faces of passing citizens.

"As Mr. Tom is tucked away in that wee basket, I'm guessing, ma'am, you have seen the roaming fortune hunters? There was an article in the newspaper that's bringing them in."

Ella nodded grimly, tutting to herself at the mention of Axel's classified advert. "It's our reason for this extra caution today." And Tom wriggled back down inside the basket. "We thank you for your concern."

"Awful lot of money..." Cheapcuts said from the box, a wistful edge to his voice, as he squinted into the distance. "Money turns even wise men to fools, that's what me Ma said."

Dirk doffed his tricorn hat to his breastbone in a gesture of earnestness that echoed his young apprentice. "I'm sure no *loyal* citizen will be tempted," the coachman said stoically.

Ella bit her lip. And lack of money drove many good people to desperate measures. "Speaking of finances and bad luck, Hansel is overseeing the town's books. He told me many workers have been dismissed or those that remain are working without pay. If you know of anyone in such circumstances, can you please let me know? I will see if the castle kitchens can feed the families." Ella glanced at the castle rooftops in the distance with the mountain range behind them. Last month, her sister had suggested the wing of the castle Ella had formerly occupied could be shut down to save money. Now, that seemed wise, all things considered, but she would have to make sure the castle staff were not thrown out on the street.

She sighed. "If only I had more than one flying carpet to sell and help raise funds, Like I did for Doctor Hyde's hospital..."

"Speaking of the good doctor, that's the reason we stopped to chat," Dirk said, and placed his tricorn squarely back on his head. "Word is, Doctor Hyde is looking for you, ma'am. Regarding witnessing some terrible accident? Apparently, he's quite intent on speaking to you as soon as possible."

The coachman gestured to the ornate carriage. "We can drive you to the Hot Cockle Lane charity hospital now if that suits, ma'am? We have time before fetching her Highness for the formal engagements with them mayoral candidates later in the day."

"Really? The tragic incident this morning? When the mayoral candidate was knocked down?" Ella stood back, perplexed, wondering what Doctor Hyde wanted to ask her. Surely she knew nothing more than anyone else who had witnessed Bertram's death? It was a mystery.

CHAPTER II

DOCTOR HYDE'S LABORATORY

ALONG WITH THE REPAIRS TO the roof, there were several signs of improvements in the former warehouse building on Hot Cockle Lane that now housed the town's charity hospital. Though most of the obvious changes were frugal with an emphasis on functionality. One such being an old desk and chair placed just inside the entrance to create a reception area.

Marge, the midwife, was stationed at the desk, flipping through a copy of the *Nottingham News*. She looked up briefly, disinterest plastered across her pretty doll features, but her dull boredom suddenly vanished as her blue eyes sparked with enthusiasm and she jumped to her feet, nearly knocking the rickety chair over. "Lady Ella! How lovely to see you..." Marge peered behind Ella, as if seeking *something* or expecting *someone* to be standing behind Ella, "Not travelling with that lovely cat of yours today...?" Marge's eyes glanced back at the newspaper on her desk, and Ella swallowed.

Oh dear... As far as Ella could remember, Tomcat had never spoken or revealed he could talk in front of the little midwife, but Marge was shrewd and a collector of gossip. Had the woman put two and two together and realised the talking cat Axel was hunting was supposedly Ella's cat?

Marge knelt down to tie her already firmly knotted boot strings while peering at the toes of Ella's own stout walking boots peeping out from the hem of her long woollen skirts.

Ella leaned on the handle of Sally's trolley, in which Tomcat remained safely hidden. "Doctor Hyde wants to speak with me?"

Marge sighed, her interest waning now Ella didn't have what she wanted, and she pointed across the warehouse floor, past rows of patients' beds, at a heavy door on the back wall. "Yes, he's in there. In his laboratory. Follow the smell." Marge's eyes narrowed, now fixed on the wicker basket, and her eagerness reappeared. She made a grab for Ella's shopping basket, adding, "Don't keep the doctor waiting. I will keep an eye on your shopping. No point dragging this behind you!"

Ella drew back, clutched the duck-head carved handle of Sally's trolley tightly. "Thank you, but no. It steadies my balance," Ella said, shooing the little midwife away. "It's like having a second walking stick. I prefer to keep it with me."

"I was only trying to help," Marge sniped, sounding affronted, while casting openly curious appraisal of the trolley. "It wasn't like I was going to *look through* your basket..."

Ha! Ella thought sourly as she wheeled the trolley across the flagstones, wincing at the squeak that had definitely worsened. At least Goldi had given her temporary relief from the pain in her knees. Should she have to make a quick escape today, her arthritic joints wouldn't slow her down...

Ella raised her knuckles, but the laboratory door opened suddenly. A waft of foul, fishy air released from the room, along with Doctor Hyde. His typically dour expression and hawkish features blossomed with keen interest. "Mistress Charming, excellent! Do come in, forgive the odour. I'm concluding some experiments." He gestured to the thick leather apron worn over his black duster coat. And then the tall thin doctor bustled her into the bland but functional space, which was mostly dedicated to a long wooden work bench laden with all manner of items.

There were rows of small glass vials which Ella recognised as test tubes, and the vials surrounded a central jar that appeared to be filled with black onions. Various strips of colour paper hung pegged above the test tubes, numbers correlating to the vials below. Also nestled on the crowded workbench was a silver coffee pot, bubbling and steaming away. Coffee was a rare and expensive beverage in these parts, and the doctor was the only person Ella knew who brewed their own. While the pleasant aroma of coffee usually dominated the doctor's office; here in this laboratory space, the coffee competed with a mysteriously strong odour akin to rotting fish.

Ella sought her pockets for a fresh handkerchief and clamped the cotton to her face. "Gracious, what are you pickling?" The mixture of scents was most peculiar, and very unpleasant, like spoiled seaweed. Her gaze locked on the large central glass jar. Now that she looked closely, were the black onions...wriggling?

"These are my leeches!" Hyde enthused, aglow with scientific curiosity. "Such clever little fellows. I feed them a diet of fermented herring..." But on seeing Ella's reaction, Hyde's dour looks returned and he apologised. "I confess, I've grown immune to the smell, and I forget how pungent they are." He raised a finger as if he had a good idea. He up-ended an old coal bucket that was being used as a wastepaper basket for discarded test tube strips, and lowered the bucket over the glass jar of black wriggling leeches.

Ella gulped and pushed the vision of the jar's contents from her mind as the doctor adjusted the flame under the coffee pot to encourage the clouds of steam to help cover up the other odours. "Coffee?" he asked. "Freshly brewed? I assure you the taste is not affected." He gestured to a large cantilever bellows. "The bellows will draw the foul odour away in a moment too."

"Thank you," Ella said, and wheeled the trolley to the far side of the room beside his desk laden with medical instruments and textbooks. Hyde pulled out a chair for her in front of the small rickety desk so she could sit, and then proceed to pump the noisy foot-operated bellows.

While Hyde's back was turned, Tomcat peeped his fluffy white head up from the basket, both paws clamped to his nose, and he whispered to Ella, "Can I *please* come out? I'm suffocating!"

Ella pursed her lips, undecided. Doctor Hyde *had* witnessed Tomcat talking last month while they were at the auction selling the flying carpet and a foreign buyer had exclaimed over the value of such a cat. But Tom and Hyde hadn't been *officially* introduced. Where did the doctor's loyalties lie?

Doctor looked over his shoulder from the bellows, and spying Tomcat, hurriedly closed his laboratory door. "Please, allow me..." He cleared a space for Tom to sit on the desk, adding, "I am glad to have this opportunity to talk freely." He leaned over the desk and pointed in the general direction of the hospital ward beyond. "It has come to my attention that the sheriff is seeking your extraordinary cat..." He squared his black duster collar. "I assure you, discretion is my middle name."

Tomcat grinned. "Discretion is Ella's middle name too!"

The doctor tipped his head, confused, and Ella shrugged. Strictly speaking, Tom was correct. "Ella Discretion Fortitude Gertrude Charming, to be precise."

The doctor made a perfunctory bow and then attended to the bubbling coffee urn and poured two cups of black coffee, and, much to her surprise, provided a saucer of cream for Tom. But then, the doctor must have been expecting them as he had spread word he needed to talk to her.

"The first thing I'm going to do when I'm human and have thumbs again is, I am going to pick up *everything* I see!" Tomcat muttered to himself and then daintily licked the cream, his little pink tongue lapping the saucer clean.

Ella sipped the hot coffee, thick and dark the way the doctor liked it, and raised her eyebrows at him. "You wanted to see me?"

"Yes, right, to the business of the day." Doctor Hyde took the cue and steepled his fingers. "You are wondering why I asked you here. Quite simply, I require a reliable eyewitness account of Bertram's accident. I was informed you were among the crowd at the time of his death."

"Yes, though I did not have a direct line of sight." Ella set the cup down. "Was there something untoward in what people said?"

Hyde held up a finger. "In a manner of speaking. Things do not add up. From what I have been told and by my own observations of the deceased—from what my autopsy, and what my clever little fellows have deduced." He cast a fond gaze towards the rusty coal bucket covering the stinky jar. "Being struck by a horse and cart doesn't align with the true cause of Bertram's death."

Chapter 12

What the Doctor Deduced

Tomcat stood up, hackles raised. "Oh! Do you think he was poisoned?" Tomcat hitched a paw at a hardbound copy of the book *Rare Poisons and their Antidotes*, which the doctor had authored and was lying open over on the workbench. "You were the one who realised the former mayor had been poisoned last month!"

Ella sat forward. "And you hope I might have seen something others didn't? Like, for example, someone slipping him poison?" A vision of Bertram shouting at his son Spalding, *'You'll be an actor over my dead body...'* darted to the forefront of her mind. "Or that I am aware of a hidden motive?"

Hyde waved off her suggestions. "If you please, Mistress Charming. I would be grateful if you recount *only* what you saw, paying careful attention to observed accurate details. Try to leave nothing out, but please don't, er, add anything in. No embellishments. I wish to hear the facts." He sat back, eyes closed, listening intently.

Tomcat's whiskers fanned. Ella had mentioned the doctor's unique talents, that Hyde had his own method of deduction. Tom was no doubt curious to see this line of questioning in action. Ella thought back on what she witnessed that morning...

A few minutes later, after hearing her account, Hyde sucked air in over his teeth and sat up straight. He looked disappointed.

"That doesn't match with your conclusion...?" She glanced toward the bench top of medical equipment and the rotting fish smell emanating from the coal bucket into the room.

"No." The doctor ran a hand over his balding head, a gesture of frustration. He sat forward and lowered his voice, "There was clear ligature bruising around the deceased's neck."

"Ligature bruising?" Ella raised an eyebrow. "Strangulation?" Ella was stunned. While many people jumped to conclusions, the doctor was not among them. "Go on, we're listening."

Doctor Hyde grimaced. "My tests at this stage point to something...unusual. Which is why I wanted to hear what you had witnessed, so I might rule in—or out—the possibility some of Bertram's clothing became caught in a carriage wheel."

Ella thought over the scene again. "Let me think... Bertram had been arguing moments before, with both his actor son, Spalding, and his political opponent, the accountant, Jacob Marley."

In her mind's eye, she saw Marley, with his hands around Bertram's neck, shaking him. "Is it possible the bruising occurred *after* death? By hands placed around Bertram's throat, *after* he was being knocked down?"

Hyde shook his head. "The bruising was uniform, a solid line, if you will." He curled his hand in demonstration. "Fingers create pressure points. It leaves a distinct pattern. Plus, it would have to have been done by someone fit and strong—this happened swiftly. Which is why I suggested an item of clothing caught in a wheel."

"Oh, Bertram's tie! The red one!"

"A tie? There was no such item when the body was brought in." Hyde looked encouraged. He curled a fist in triumph. "Yes, that could be the missing factor! Pulled taut, crushed his windpipe. That could explain the markings!"

Ella sat back. "But, no, I distinctly recall the red cravat on his person after he went down."

"You're sure they removed the cravat *after* Bertram fell—it wasn't caught and ripped off by the wheel?"

"I don't recall *if* it was removed, just that there was a discussion between Fairweather and Mr. Beau that his cravat *should* be loosened. I am certain it was neatly affixed when he went down. The ends were tucked under his waistcoat and there were no long flapping tails to get caught in spokes."

"Hmm." Hyde's brows creased in deep thought.

Oh dear. Ella wondered, was the good doctor doubting her ability to observe accurate details and her future reliability as a witness? It was all very odd and something strange was going on, but she knew what she saw. She didn't doubt her own eyes. The tie was about Bertram's neck before he fell. She pictured him gasping, having jumped clear of one carriage, straight into the path of the second. And the red tie was neat about his neck when he was on the ground and everyone crowded around to offer assistance.

Hyde's gaze was drawn to the upturned coal bucket. He took a breath, as if having come to a decision. "What I'm about to reveal must not leave this room..." Ella nodded, and Tom mimed stitching his lips. Hyde sat forward. "Whatever caused the ligature bruising on Bertram's neck also left a telltale trace of black magic on his skin."

Ella gasped, drawing in a sharp breath. "Black magic!"

The doctor stood and gestured to the strips of paper pegged above the test tubes. Some papers were stained yellow or brown, but one strip was vivid crimson. Without touching the piece of paper, he said, "My leeches extracted this. Though miniscule, there was a fresh and potent element of black magic in Bertram's bloodwork."

"Of course. That explains the smell in here—It's not from the leeches eating pickled herrings. It's the awful taint of black magic!" Tom stood bolt upright.

"Magic preserve!" Ella cried, astonished to learn black magic was involved in Bertram's death. No wonder the doctor wanted to hear her account of the supposed accident. "Doctor! You imply it was no accident? Bertram was murdered!"

CHAPTER 13

DOCTOR HYDE'S REVELATION

"IF BERTRAM'S DEATH WAS NOT an accident, then we must uncover the culprit! Where do we begin?" Ella muttered to herself. Catching a killer was no simple task. Who would want Bertram dead?

As if reading her thoughts, Tomcat asked, "Does Bertram have any enemies? Real enemies?"

"None that I know of," Ella admitted. "All I can think of right now are his public rivals—Marley for one—and I can't believe he or another candidate for mayor would *kill* for the position. Surely not?"

Tom's intense green eyes blinked up at her, concern and sympathy readable as his whiskers drooped.

"If I may, locating the tie must be the top priority," Hyde interjected pragmatically. "Though on the surface you have given me the missing piece of the puzzle, I must inspect and test the red cravat you spoke of to confirm our working theory. That the tie was the source of the black magic residue on Bertram's skin..." Hyde gestured to several books and notes spilling open on his bench, like he had been searching for an answer. "Because without indisputable proof that the tie could provide, I can only conclude that though the gentleman was knocked down by a horse and hit by a hoof and a carriage wheel, the true cause of death was affixation from strangulation, causes 'unknown'." He looked at Ella. "Do you know how a strangulation death might even be invoked via black magic?"

Ella swallowed, and unconsciously rubbed her throat. "Yes, I'm afraid I do. There is a rather nasty spell—called the Hangman's Knot. It had a benign beginning, originally used in sailors' spells—to keep knots firm, that sort of thing. But when combined with black magic, the Hangman's Knot spell can turn ropes, ties, scarves, any fabric really, into a sort of living knot. Once the bewitched item is placed about a neck and a knot tied, the knot gets tighter and tighter, until death occurs."

"Nasty," Hyde muttered. He nodded to himself. "So the tie itself *could* indeed be a murder weapon and source of the black magic on the deceased's skin... Good. Thank you. Mistress Charming, your expertise is enlightening." He bowed, and Ella felt a flush of warmth at his compliment.

"I feel this *Hangman's Knot* spell is a strong possibility," the doctor continued. "Particularly as the 'run over' doesn't explain the 'strangled' complication without his tie or clothing being caught by the carriage wheel."

He gestured to the coloured strips of paper. "See here. After the witnesses' recollections did not account for the bruising on the neck, and having seen an increase in magical poisonings, I felt compelled to test the body. Using my leeches, I conducted separate tests on body and clothing. Black magic residue was on his skin, directly under the ligature bruising—but crucially *not* in his stomach contents. The deceased is out on a slab of ice in the next building. I can show you precisely how my tests are done, if you wish? The leeches are quite fascinating to watch."

Ella clamped the handkerchief to her face again. "No, thank you! I will take your word for it." She drew a short breath, trying not to breathe in the rancid seaweed air that had filled the laboratory once more.

Tomcat's tail was beginning to droop. "It is making me a bit woozy," he uttered, clamping a paw across his snout. "I thought it was because of the fermented herrings, but it probably is the black magic residue."

Ella blanched, grabbing up a manilla folder, she fanned the air. "Tom is allergic to black magic! Can you please operate the bellows again?"

"Let us vacate the laboratory all together. Follow me, this way, there is a small balcony outback, overhanging the river," Doctor Hyde said, getting to his feet and gesturing to a side door at the top of a small flight of stone steps, "from when the hospital was a warehouse. We might discuss this matter outside there..."

They followed the doctor up the steps and a blast of wintery air and noises from the industry of Hot Cockle Lane greeted them out on the balcony overhanging the frozen river. Outside, the air, though crisp, in truth, was not as fresh as other parts of the town. Down here in the river district, the prime industry of Hot Cockle Lane was the fish smoking works.

Tom jumped down from Ella's arms, sucked in big lungfuls of air and exclaimed loudly, "That is better!"

Hyde stood beside the cat, and oddly repeated Tom's words, and then stretched with exaggeration. "That is so much better! Fresh air is what I needed." He nodded covertly at the dozens of people working outside on the river, hauling barrels, as well as several children ice-skating, and Ella grasped the reason for the doctor's odd mimicry of Tom. The river was a busy area. A passing fortune hunter wouldn't believe their luck if standing across on the dock at that moment and caught sight of the talking cat.

While Tom breathed deeply and recovered, Ella turned the moments leading up to Bertram's death again over in her mind. "I will help find the tie," she said aloud to Hyde. "Someone might have removed it while trying to revive Bertram. Most likely, they put it in their pocket for safekeeping. I will start by talking to the witnesses."

"Splendid plan," Hyde concurred, leaning on the balcony railing. "Until the tie is located and tested, my official report will have to state the death as accidental." He sighed. "Unfortunately, I am too busy to assist you in searching for the tie. There is an increase in magic-related poisoning cases following the month of magical amnesty." He gestured to the hospital building at their back, and Ella recalled all the case books and notes spilling open on his workbench. "There is much work to be done."

"An increase in magical poisonings?" Ella said, thinking back on her conversation with Goldilocks. "Goldi also said something similar this morning. Perhaps you should compare notes with her?"

"That is a capital idea," Hyde agreed. "Pool resources."

"We can ask Robinne or Olly to help us look for the tie!" Tomcat whispered. "Maybe Cass…although I guess she'll be busy with her last day of work or packing to leave on the barge tomorrow…"

"Yes, and we better be swift in locating it," Ella stated, with a sense of foreboding as she thought back to the morning's events. "Before Spalding or the other actors start rumours spreading that Bertram's death is attributed to the supposed curse of the *Lady MacDeath* play."

"I'm sorry, I'm not familiar with that?" Hyde frowned.

"Nor me," added Tom, his tail flicking across the stone steps.

Ella quickly explained. "You see, just before Bertram was struck down, Nigella announced her theatre company will perform *Lady MacDeath*—most of the cast were appalled, Spalding—Bertram's son', not least of all."

She recalled the argument the pair were having moments before Bertram's death. *'You'll be an actor over my dead body!'*

"Poor Spalding was traumatised by seeing his father knocked over. I am sure he thought Nigella choosing to put on the so-called cursed *Lady MacDeath* play had tempted fate. Actors are a very superstitious lot. To break the curse and ensure a successful season, three—no, four. Four deaths *supposedly* have to occur before opening night. These deaths represent four tragic deaths from people involved in the play in the past. The first person to die was trampled."

"Ahh. I see, just as what happened—or rather, *appeared*—to happen Bertram," Hyde comprehended grimly.

Ella nodded. "Curse rumours must be stamped out quickly, or people will see curses, morning, lunch and tea!"

"But how can you not believe in the opening night curse when you know black magic is real?" Tom wanted to know.

"Tosh. It's not a *proper* curse," Ella said. "Playhouse superstitions are nonsense from overactive imaginations, nothing more. Curses back in my day, I tell you, were truly harrowing—no rhymes or silly hand gestures of Mr. Beau!"

Tom looked intrigued. "A rhyme? And what hand gesture thing did Mr. Beau show you? How did it go?"

Ella demonstrated and shuddered. "The original playhouse deaths sixty years ago, which spurned the 'curse' superstition, weren't because of black magic at all, but I recall it certainly was a tragic collection of events."

Tom blinked. "Wait? You *remember*? I forget how truly old you are. Remind me again, how old are you?"

Ella just glowered at him.

Hyde coughed politely. "But you knew all those people? The original four who died at the playhouse?"

Ella responded tightly. "Yes, I did, and I empathised and grieved with their families—gosh! Mr. Beau. I am certain one of his great uncles was a victim!" She drummed a finger, deep and thought. "Hmm...I wager that it must have been Ebenezer, who drowned in the bath."

Hyde blanched, clearly surprised. "Drowned in the bath?"

"Yes. Although there was debate whether he simply *expired* while taking his bath—the man was in poor health and a terrible old drunk..." She glanced up over at the back door as from within the hospital shouting echoed.

"Who is in charge here?" An angry voice called out from within the hospital. "I demand to speak to the highest authority! Out of my way!" The female voice commanded, and a second later, the back door banged open. Marge, all in a flap, rushed out up to the top of the steps, and tried to hold back an agitated, beautiful woman, possibly in her late forties or early fifties.

Ella had seen the woman before, just a month ago, at the afternoon tea held to honour her brother Merlin. She—Catherine?—had been the hostess. Catherine, yes, that was her name, Ella recalled now. Catherine was Spalding's mother and Bertram's wife...

Though dressed in stylish furs and with a flattering tailor-made coat, an air of distress made her unkempt, her cheeks red and her mascara smudged. "My husband!" the woman said, pushing up behind Marge, who dug in her heels, flung her arms out to body block the woman, blurted, "Mr. Bertram's wife, Doctor Hyde! Came to claim the gentleman's body!"

"Rogue! Thief!" the accusations spilled in breathy anguish from the recent widow's pale lips, her eyes red raw. "This is not to be born! He is dead *and robbed*? I demand you attend to this matter at once! Where are my husband's belongings? The silk cravat is missing! Who has stolen his red silk cravat? Was it you?"

CHAPTER 14

TOM AND ELLA TALK TACTICS

A TENSE FEW MINUTES PASSED while Marge and Hyde—one dragging, one escorting—the hysterical widow away to Hyde's office so they might discuss the matter in privacy. As if everyone within a mile radius hadn't heard the outrageous accusations, Ella thought sourly, as she excused herself and escaped the hospital with Tomcat.

Ella and Tom walked along the frozen river edge, rather than weaving along the dockyard alleyways back towards the northern side of town. As though chilly, the river had fewer strangers about.

"Right, we shall do our part and find that missing tie so Doctor Hyde can conduct his tests for black magic," Ella instructed Tom, as she towed the trolley after her across the thick white ice. "It was preposterous of Catherine to think that Hyde—or anyone—would steal from the deceased."

"Who else was there when Spalding's dad was knocked down?" Tom asked.

Ella rubbed her chin thoughtfully, recalling the scene. "The main three I recall were Jacob Marley, Mr. Beau and Mistress Fairweather... Actually, Nigella was there too. Any of them could have taken it without thinking. I expect whoever loosened it simply popped it in their pocket."

Tom's whiskers fanned. "Spalding too. You did say he was there? What if he took it?"

Ella shook her head. "I doubt that. Surely then the widow wouldn't be in such an outcry."

"Speaking of people behaving oddly..." Tom's tail dipped as if he'd had a nasty thought. "Didn't you say something about Jacob Marley actually wrapping his hands about the gentleman's throat? That's an odd thing to do when someone is hurt."

"True—although Marley was very upset and shocked. They'd been bickering only seconds before, and to suddenly have your political opponent at your mercy..." Ella shook off the uncharitable thought. "But yes, Marley is likely to have seen what happened to the tie. He has an office in the wing of the town hall. Shall we head there first or carry on to Haversham's academy? Don't forget, we were going to the library for any reference books that might forewarn what will happen to your memories when you transform back into your real body."

"I haven't forgotten..." He looked away, an air of dejection and grave concern crossing his feline features. "...but I think finding the tie is more urgent. Not only so it can be tested for black magic, but because that lady pretty much accused Doctor Hyde of stealing the tie from her dead husband!"

Ella wheeled the shopping basket around and opened the lid. "Pop yourself in the trolley. We have to leave the riverside here and venture back up onto the street, and we don't want to risk an altercation with any of Axel's crossbow-toting fortune hunters."

Tomcat did as bid and sprang into Sally's basket. The wicker creaked as he settled into place. "This trolley is like my own personal carriage!"

"I suppose that makes me the horse," Ella said, peering inside before lowering the basket flap that covered the opening. "Comfy?"

"Snug and secure," Tomcat replied and added, "Giddy up!"

"Hilarious, Tom..."

They set off across the cobblestone, but with Tom's added weight, one of the trolley wheels started squeaking at once. "Oops! I forgot about that!" The basket flap raised as Tomcat's ears peeped out of the trolley. "Will the sound attract unwanted attention?"

"Not as much as a cat peeping out the top and asking questions." Ella pushed the basket lid closed and nudged him back inside. "I admit the squeak is not ideal, but it's not like anyone is tracking us. So long as no one knows there's a cat in the squeaky trolley, no one will think anything of it."

"Okay," Tomcat said, sounding unconvinced, and readjusting his position by turning around and around in the basket.

"Is everything all right?" Ella frowned when he didn't settle. "I thought you said it was comfy in there?"

"It was, but I dislodged something. I think I'm sitting on an apple. It's buried under the newspaper. Hold on."

The basket rustled and shook and Ella stood and tried to remain nonchalant as a few people wandered past, giving her sideways glances. Suddenly, the basket flap flopped open, and an apple popped out onto the cobbles, followed by a banana.

"Oh, that's wasteful!" Ella grumbled, stooping to retrieve the fruit as the apple bounced, rolled down the street and slid towards a gutter, when the sound of shimmering bells made her bolt upright. "Sibylla!" Ella looked left and right, unsure which avenue the bells were echoing down. The last thing she wanted was to run into her sister on her way to receive the official announcements of the mayoral candidates—that was exactly the tedious type of council duty that Sibylla would gladly fob off onto Ella.

"Hold on tight!" Ella said, gripping the duck-shaped handle of Sally's trolley and shuffled down around the corner. Yes! The avenue ahead was clear. Excellent.

Ella glanced back over her shoulder. From the queen's coach behind her, Dirk Turpin and his apprentice Cheapcuts, raised their jaunty tricorns, signalling they had spotted her. "Caught. Worse luck…"

The window sash snapped down, and a manicured fingernail, painted blood red, jabbed out at her. "You! Get in!" Sibylla's haughty 'majesty voice' intoned, and Ella schooled her face with what she hoped reflected a quiet dignity and not irritation as Cheapcuts assisted her to alight the carriage, loading her supposed shopping basket in behind her.

Chapter 15

The Queen's Has Other Plans

THE QUEEN TUCKED HER VOLUMINOUS silken skirts out of the way and cast a sour glance at Ella's shopping trolley, the snow-damp wheels dripping ice on the coach carpet. "I don't know why you conduct yourself in such a humble manner. It's unseemly. I could hear you squeaking over the horses' hooves."

"It is very good of you to stop and help," Ella said, settling into the plush velvet and fur interior, while trying to take advantage of the situation, "I'm just heading to the town hall, and a ride is most welcome!" She held out the apple and smiled winningly. "Fruit?"

Sibylla pursed her perfect lips. "Forget that. Change of plans. Your shopping or whatever will have to wait." Sibylla explained she was on her way to the town hall to accept the mayoral candidates. "The shoo-in legacy candidate was killed this morning," Sibylla added, unaware of Ella's witnessing the very event she described only a few hours beforehand. "This means the mayoral race has opened up and undoubtedly there will be a *surge* of last-minute candidates. And that means the whole thing will be *tediously long* with all their dull introductory speeches. I need you to stand in for me at the town hall. I'm chatting to Prince John via magic mirror in thirty minutes and I can't delay him." She gave Ella a frazzled look full of scorn. "Need I remind you of your oath to support me as both regent and sister?"

Ella felt a stab of guilt. Neglecting her sister or her duty was not her intention. "Of course not. I am at your service... And speaking of bad news. I'm afraid Hansel's report into the town finances is worse than either of us could have imagined. Harold wasn't stealing; he simply wasn't paying anyone. We have debt coming out of our—"

"Don't worry about all that," Sibylla interrupted, cutting Ella off. "I have resolved the money crisis. In fact, it's what I'm going to discuss with John. Finalise the details."

Ella grimaced. "If you mean that scheme to let John build his prison on Wyld soil, you promised I had until Christmas to find another way to raise the money."

Sibylla's hand waving increased. "No, no, it's nothing of the kind. We can forget John's prison, and you, too, are off the hook. Once again, I have come through and saved our fair kingdom in her hour of financial crisis."

Ella didn't recall her sister having done anything of the sort before, but she was too curious to labour the point. "Are you going to explain *how* you did it, or are you just going to be smug about it?"

"The answer is beautiful in its simplicity. We shall make our own money—*Paper money*," Sibylla exclaimed. "See? We shall adopt paper currency—it's all the rage. John was telling me about it. They're doing it in Nottingham, and so I thought why not us too? It's high tech, cutting edge."

Ella scowled. "How exactly will that work? We don't have the gold to swap for the paper kind."

"Silly! What swap nonsense are you talking about? Don't you see? Paper money is *worth* whatever you say it is."

"It is...?"

"Yes! I shall simply decree that *my* paper money is equivalent, or perhaps, worth *slightly more* than John's paper money. Don't fret, I won't be greedy. We don't want to rub his nose in it."

Ella shut her eyes. Magic preserve! "Is that really how you think paper money works? It's worth whatever *you* say it is!"

All the while, Sibylla kept casting suspicious glances at the shopping basket as it creaked, not always in time with the sway of the coach. Whatever Tom was sitting on in there must be uncomfortable, or perhaps he was trying not to laugh at Sibylla's absurd money-making scheme...

"Is something alive in there?" Sibylla narrowed her eyes. "Not harbouring a talking cat, are you?"

Ella's eyes bulged. Magic preserve! What dreadful luck! To think she'd kept Tomcat's presence hidden from Sibylla all these months, and now everything was hanging in the balance thanks to a lumpy banana! "No!" she gulped, feeling a scald of heat rise to colour her cheeks.

Sibylla rolled her eyes disdainfully. "Ha! I knew you were trying to trick me! I may never have achieved such academic magic as you, but I'm not fool enough to believe such a hoax. A talking cat loose in Charmington? Really! That ridiculous article was an embarrassment to journalistic integrity."

Ella frowned. An *article* in the paper? "Wait? What article?"

"Oh! So you didn't read it? Well then, here's some amusement for you." Sibylla sat forward and pulled out a copy of The *Nottingham Times* from the recess on the door of the coach. "In today's paper, they had the gall to report that there was a talking cat at the magical auction last month. I tell you, the *Nottingham Times* is getting ridiculous..." She flattened out the paper and read, "A businessman, Mr. Aladdin, is quoted as saying, 'The talking cat would easily fetch three times the value of the flying carpet', and, 'My master would happily pay anyone who would deliver the talking cat to him, no questions asked...'"

Sibylla tutted before continuing, and Ella listened with increasing alarm to the reported account from the auction she and Tomcat had attended last month when Ella was selling her flying carpet to raise funds for the hospital.

"Oh, good gracious!" Ella said when her sister had finished reading. Someone *must* have been listening in when she spoke to the wealthy businessman that was sent to buy the flying carpet on behalf of his employer. No wonder there were so many fortune hunters about town today. Axel's little reward notice in the classifieds *wasn't* what was attracting them—it was this full-blown speculative article!

"Magic preserve! This is the worst!" Ella hissed. "The entire kingdom will be knee-deep in fortune hunters by the end of the week!"

"I quite agree," concurred her sister, nodding along. "It's precisely the foolish sort of thing that I feared. I temporarily allow magic's use back in our kingdom for *one month*, and this happens." The queen sighed and stuffed the paper into the slot built into the carriage door. "It's almost a shame it's not true. Selling the talking cat would restore the kingdom's coffers, at least for a month or two.."

Ella was too shocked and horrified to return her sister's smile. It was no joking matter! To think this article was most likely what Dirk and Cheapcuts had been warning her about! Gosh! If only she hadn't assumed she knew what was going on and had actually listened. Her false pride might be the death of her—no, worse! Tomcat's capture!

She nudged the trolley with her boot toe, hoping that Tomcat wasn't snoozing in there but was actually listening and paying heed, because the consequences of their actions today had never been so fraught with danger.

Though Axel's bounty had value, the true value to the right buyer was worth much, much more! No doubt the professional bounty hunters would put two and two together and their plans to capture the talking cat would not have them hand Tomcat over to Axel, but rather, *sell* the talking cat to Mr. Aladdin!

An even more terrifyingly dreadful thought occurred. The fortune hunters didn't know what the cat they were looking for looked like, but... Axel...?

"Ah, I take it Sheriff Axel *hasn't* seen the article? Were you planning on bringing it to his attention?" Ella asked, feigning casual interest.

Sibylla snorted, dismissive, and laughed. "Why would I? The whole thing is clearly an absurd hoax. Think of the magic required, not only to do such a spell, but to maintain it!" She crossed her arms and leaned back against the furs. "If such a cat existed, it would need ninety lives, let alone nine lives, to survive the week. The entire kingdom would be itching to capture it..."

CHAPTER 16

MEET THE CANDIDATES

A SHORT TIME LATER, ELLA'S thoughts all in a swirl, the coach arrived at the town hall and she was bundled out onto the steps. Cheapcuts held the reins of the horses while Dirk Turpin assisted Ella up the first few steps, awkwardly bumping the trolley behind her.

"Thank you, I can manage from here," Ella assured Dirk as citizens flowed around and past her, their attention drawn by the entrance of the queen's grand coach. "Sibylla will not want to keep waiting for her appointment with Prince John..."

Dirk saluted, touching his hand to his smart tricorn. "Yes, ma'am." He cast a nervous glance at the various steely-eyed individuals slouching around the police station, all dressed in hunting cloaks and bundled up with furs. Some drank, some smoked, others played cards, as if they didn't have a care in the world and despite being barred from some of the indoor public venues, they were clearly determined to stake out the entire township. "Do take care 'o yerself, there's a lot of strangers in town this morning'. Young Cheapcuts and I will keep our ears to the ground, on account of...our mutual friend."

Ella nodded and squeezed his shoulder. Clearly Tom's friends were just as nervous as she was about what Tom's future might hold as word spread of Mr. Aladdin's plea in the newspaper: *My master would happily pay anyone who would deliver the talking cat to him, no questions asked...*

No questions asked! It was practically an open invitation to thieves! The sooner Tom had himself fitted out in Sally's clever goose hat disguise, the better.

"I must find Sally," Ella muttered aloud to herself once Dirk departed, as if mentally going about her tasks and not discussing them with anyone in particular. "See if the pretty feather *hat* she was making is ready."

A gentle *tap-tap* sound from the basket interior signalled Tomcat had received her message. Assumedly, by peeping out between the gaps in the wicker, he had drawn his own conclusions about the threat to his freedom represented by the unusual congregation of rogues and hunters loitering across the square.

Gripping the trolley handle, she ventured over to the double doors into the town hall, and sighed with relief at the familiar face on door duty.

"There you are," Robinne said, uncrossing her arms and pushing back the cowl of her distinctive red cloak. She had been leaning against the stonework, having stationed herself in the doorway of the town hall. "Do you know what's going on?" She gestured to the card players outside the police station. "Don't worry, I'm not letting *any* strangers inside. But I can't be everywhere—actually, that reminds me. Sally was looking for...you...just now. I told her to try your tax office."

Ella nodded as she dragged the squeaking trolley in behind her. "Thank you. I shall head straight there."

That would be easier said than done. The town hall foyer appeared to be *mayoral candidate central*. People milled about everywhere, indoors and out from the cold, as the population speculated over who was going to nominate themselves for mayor. Every bench seat was occupied, every alcove filled with friends and family supporting those that were putting their names down on the official ballot sheet which had been set up to record the names and on a desk at the foot of the main staircase.

Ella eyed the main staircase, teeming with people. Perhaps it would be more prudent to avoid the crowds and take the back stairs up to her tax office in the attic. Yes, that would be best. Although, dragging the trolley up the several flights by herself was not going to be easy. Goldi had relieved the pain in her knees, but that didn't mean she had any extra strength to lug the basket—especially with Tom's cat bulk inside.

She sighed and cast her gaze about, looking for another trusted face to assist her. Among several small tables which potential mayoral candidates had set up, one campaigner's booth stood noticeably unmanned. The bunting and signage remained, though the chairs were stacked neatly on top of the table and draped in a black cloth. Bertram's booth.

Bertram's main rival was situated nearby, across the oak-panelled hallway. The accountant, Jacob Marley himself, was being slapped on the back by someone, as he stood under his slogan: *Accountability matters – the numbers don't lie!*

She recalled Marley's expression that morning when he dusted off his political rival's hat. The strange mix of disgust and yet satisfaction on his face. To have his rival so suddenly knocked out of the running. Like a wish come true?

Ella shook off the thought. What mattered now was she had the perfect opportunity to question Marley about the missing tie! After all, the fellow had picked up Bertram's fallen top hat, so he might well have collected the tie if it had been loosened.

Marley bowed as Ella approached his booth, his manner professional and courteous. "Your Ladyship, good day to you. I am honoured by your presence." He made a gesture of offering her a bench seat under the window, but Ella waved off the suggestion.

Turning about, she positioned the trolley basket so inside Tom would face the corridor and not the wall. "I'm looking forward to hearing the speeches and debates of the candidates later today," Ella fibbed. "Sibylla has been called away, so I will stand in her stead for this time-honoured tradition."

Marley bowed again and Ella squinted at the blue silk cravat he wore. It was the same style, or appeared very similar to the red one Bertram himself had been wearing.

"I confess my own enjoyment of the day will be greatly lessened," Marley said. "I had been looking forward to the verbal sparring and matching my wits against Bertram. It will not be the same without him..." The accountant's face creased, a look of genuine grief creased his cleanly shaven features. "Bertram and I have been rivals for a lifetime...I never thought that would end."

"Oh, yes?" Ella said, encouraging him to talk since he seemed wanting to share. "Rivals?"

Marley smoothed his suit jacket. "Oh yes, since boyhood. And when we were young men, we both were enchanted by the lovely Catherine." His jaw clenched, and he coughed. "At the time, I thought I would never forgive him for stealing her away, but I was young and arrogant. But...er, now I admit, Bertram made Catherine very happy."

Ella clasped the man's hand and patted it sympathetically. "Ah yes, the wisdom that one acquires with age." She leaned back and glanced over at Bertram's booth draped in black. "Speaking of Bertram, I don't suppose you know what happened to the fine cravat he was wearing this morning at the time of the accident? I saw you were kind enough to collect his top hat, and I thought you might have also found the cravat?"

Marley's brow creased, and he let go of her hands suddenly, but then recovered his surprise and looked genuinely confused. "Why, no. I don't remember seeing a cravat."

Ella tilted her head slightly. "It was red. Silk, I believe. Similar, if not identical, to your own."

Marley's hands went as of their own volition to his throat and he touched the blue silk at his neck. He swallowed and shook his head again. "Oh, yes, vaguely, I recall." He shook his head firmly and straightened his stance. "But I haven't seen it, I am sure he was still wearing it when, er..." He wiped his brow. "They stretchered him away. Forgive me, I must..." He bowed and backed away, striding off down the corridor and disappeared within the crowd.

Ella narrowed her eyes. "Hmm, so, Marley and Bertram were long-standing rivals..." And there was no doubt she said something which unsettled him. Was he hiding something, or was it just grief? Certainly, the abrupt death of a lifelong rival would leave a gaping hole in one's sense of identity.

Her gaze returned to the banners and slogans that draped Marley's campaigning booth. *Accountability matters! The numbers don't lie!*

Many had touted Bertram as a shoo-in to become the next mayor, so Marley, as his rival, would have wished no sweeter revenge than 'stealing' that position out from under Bertram. But to take it without an honourable 'fight' via the ballot boxes? Could Marley be the sort of person to ensure his victory at any price?

CHAPTER 17

CLAUDE GETS ELLA'S VOTE

ELLA GRIPPED THE TROLLEY AND turned and walked along the corridor, heading towards the back staircase. Her contemplative thoughts dissipated in recognising Harold Harper among the candidates roaming the halls.

Harold, the former postmaster, who had been removed from his post two months ago due to falsifying the post office's bookkeeping—the extent of which Hansel had reported to her only that morning—was in his customary tight grey waistcoat that hid the corset he used to shape his girth. He was also wearing a new wig in a conservative brown shade that sat somewhere on the colour wheel between otter and mouse, and had a poster which touted: *Tradition! Tradition! Tradition!*

Ella rolled her eyes, but Harold wasn't the only one who appeared to be capitalising on the opportunity of Bertram's tragic death. Judging from the number of booths, clearly there was fresh interest in the mayoral election with the unfortunate demise of the frontrunner. Several hopefuls had banners and flags strung about little home-made candidate booths from where they handed out flyers, or heartily shook hands with well-wishers.

One such individual, in the middle of canvassing the townsfolk, was welcomely familiar. The attractive, smiling features of Claude stood out further along the corridor. Dressed in a smart navy blue suit, he cut a stylish and imposing figure among the curious gawking onlookers.

Unlike the other campaigners, the bookstore proprietor Claude didn't have a banner with a slogan over his table. *Whatever was his platform? Good looks and sells books?* Ella thought idly to herself, casting an appraising look as the tall, attractive Frenchman worked the town hall foyer. Shaking hands, meeting people's eyes and always giving off the air that whoever he was speaking to had his full and undivided attention. Perhaps simply being attractive and attentive *was* his strategy? She shrugged. She'd seen worse plans before. Not that *she* would ever fall for something so obvious...

"Ella, mademoiselle!" Claude said, catching her eye suddenly and gliding through the people to her, like she was the only one in the room. He clasped her hand in his strong, tanned, manly hands and pressed it to his gentle lips.

Ella gulped. Heat rising to her cheeks. She gave herself a mental shake and withdrew her hand, but slowly, so as not to give offence, and not because she enjoyed the sensation of those warm and tender lips on her skin... Another mental shake followed and she blurted out the first thing that came to mind, "Are you running for mayor?"

The attractive bookshop owner, and former stage actor, bowed, acknowledging that it was true. His smile, deep and earnest, as if she had said the most wise and astute observation rather than an awkward conclusion of a simpleton.

"But how will you have time? I thought Nigella cast you as the male lead in *Lady MacDeath*?"

"Ella, you are freezing. Here, allow me..." Claude, still holding her hand, drew her in close to him, and pressed the hand to his heart. He whispered, "I confess, I have a secret reason for entering the mayoral race... It is quite ungallant of me, I fear..."

Ella gulped, the scent of his cologne in her lungs. It was...mesmerising... "Uh..."

"If I *wrap* myself within the *embrace* of politics," Claude's melodic French accent washed over her in the intimacy of their shared physical space, and he tipped his dark head towards where Nigella herself was situated chatting with someone further down the corridor. "I cannot be...*unwrapped*...in the arms of less enticing embraces..."

"Uh..." Ella's distracted thoughts collided for a moment. Was Claude implying he *didn't* want to be cast in the play? Why ever not? Was he worried about the curse? Gosh, he had long eyelashes...

"You will...keep my roguish secret?" He smiled, expression earnest, and pressed his lips to her hand once more. "Forgive my...ungentlemanly...behaviour?"

"Uh... you, my vote! Ah, I mean, ahem. You...you have my vote," Ella stuttered, and she withdrew, stumbled a step back as his presence departed into the crowd. Dazed, Ella turned about on the spot, until snickering coming from her shopping trolley brought her back to her senses like a mental slap, and she remembered, regretfully, she wasn't allowed to cast a vote.

Ella blinked, and trying to restore her dignity, wiped the palms of hands on her skirts. It was safe to say, Claude didn't need a platform.

She reached for the trolley handle when young Olly swooped in under her arm, in a flash of golden velvet, and took control of the trolley, saying, "Missus Sally has got your *special* fancy hat ready upstairs in your office. Do you want to try it on?"

"Uh, yes, please." Ella coughed. Focusing her mind on the important tasks at hand. Tom's goose hat disguise that Sally was crafting. Yes. That was the order of the hour—that and speaking to any of the witnesses of Bertram's accident. She hadn't forgotten she had to locate the missing tie both to help clear Hyde's name and determine if it was the source of the black magic tainting Bertram's blood results. "Actually, if you please, Olly. Would you help take my er, shopping up to my tax office? The stairs are rather troublesome for me when the basket is...full."

Olly grinned at the basket in which Tomcat was hiding. "My pleasure Missus." Off they trotted, the squeaky wheel of the trolley echoing down the hall.

Ella was a step behind the youngster when Harold Harper cut across her path. Drawing breath, he said, "I believe you owe me an apology."

"Whatever for?" Ella uttered sourly, and waved young Olly to carry on without her. She turned to glare at the former postmaster.

"You accused me of stealing," Harold said loudly, attracting the attention of several bystanders, including Marley's supporters. "Smeared my good name through the mud."

Ella narrowed her eyes. "I did no such thing. I discovered you *were* keeping two sets of ledgers—you *were* *falsifying* the post office accounts. The only mud cast was from your own digging."

The onlookers chuckled at this report and Harold flapped his arms, as if highly offended by the truth. "But no money was taken!" He turned as if entreating the citizens. "I was merely endeavouring to maintain standards, uphold the faith in the town's—nay! The *kingdom's* finances. I should be rewarded for protecting the reputation of the crown." He spun back to Ella, emboldened by his own bluster, pointed at her and blurted, "You jolly well owe me an apology and a *medal!*"

Ella gritted her teeth, about to snap, "Out of my way, you loathsome toad!" when she caught sight of the political onlookers smirking and instead she forced out a smile, and in her most official and royal tone said, "Very well. I shall go fetch one from my big box of medals right now. Wait here…"

The audience tittered as Harold was left in the hallway, blinking and disorientated. But after a second, he tugged the hem of his waistcoat and puffed out his chest as if vindicated, until Marley's cohorts, chuckling behind their hands, scoffed, "I don't think she's coming back, old chap!"

• • • •

REALLY! Harold was an oaf. The nerve of that man to think he should be *rewarded* for what he did. As if hiding the truth of the post office's dire finances was a noble deed when he had stopped paying the maintenance staff!

His actions were partly responsible for the decay in the plumbing and gas lines that ultimately had forced her to shut the theatre down this morning. Imagine if that came to light? How would someone like Nigella feel if she were privy to that information? She wouldn't be in favour of offering him a medal either. She would demand Harold be flogged in the public square!

Muttering to herself at the irritation that was Harold, truly under her skin, the sight of Nigella and Mistress Fairweather ducking through a doorway into the ballroom, jerked Ella out from the depth of her mental stew. Hyde's task! Nigella or Fairweather! Had one of them removed Bertram's tie?

Ella turned about on the spot. Behind her the passage was full, while ahead it was quiet. It would only take a minute to ask the theatre director and the Baker Street orphanage matron, then she could continue around to the back of the town hall and go up to her tax office. Thank the stars that Goldi had given her poor old knees a magical dose of the pain relief—she needn't dread the climb up several flights today.

Ella pushed the door open into the ballroom. The large space appeared to be in the midst of being set up for supper later. She spied the bakers Willow and Bron, across the hall at a buffet table. Willow specialised in making delicious cakes, fudge and brownies, while Bron made all manner of bread and loaves. They must be working together to provide food for the evening's event.

There was no sign of Nigella now, but Mistress Fairweather, however, was wagging her finger at both bakers. "It's simply not hygienic! A werewolf and a dog-owner, doing the catering! No one wants fur floating in their teacups."

On seeing Ella, Willow's eyes lit up. "I'm sure this can be resolved," the young woman said, beckoning Ella with the air of a flustered professional trying to get their job done under a tight deadline.

"Whatever seems to be the matter?" Ella asked as the orphanage matron, hands on hips, tapped her toe against the polished wooden floorboards, about to launch into another litany of complaints.

Ella leaned back a little to peer at Bron and Willow, and signalled she would take care of it. Though it was true Willow owned Mr. Puddles, the wee poodle who accompanied Dirk Turpin on the queen's coach during the daytime, she was fairly sure neither baker was a werewolf.

Willow just rolled her eyes and peeled off to finish setting out the cutlery while Bron pleaded. "I'm not a werewolf! That was a rumour!"

"Mistress Fairweather," Ella attempted to intervene, drawing up her height and prepared to use her royal bossy voice as had worked so effectively on Harold, "Have no fears. Let me offer you assurance everything will run to your exacting standards. My sister, Queen Sibylla, personally sent me to ensure this important event goes ahead without delay—"

"Oh, I am honoured, your Ladyship!" Fairweather snapped open her ostrich feather and fluttered it. "And you are so right! The ballroom is the perfect place in which to host the play! Do me the honour and take a turn with me about the room!"

Mistress Fairweather slipped her arm under Ella's like they were old friends, and dragged her about the room, as if they weren't standing in the large empty ballroom among the round tables draped with crisp white linen, but were two fashionable ladies strolling along a promenade. "We can easily fit an audience here," the matron said, using her ostentatious fan as a pointer while Willow and Bron, with relieved sighs, returned to the pressing business of getting everything ready. "And the dais platform shall become the stage! How clever you are! That wretched Beau won't rain on my parade! As they say, the show must go on!"

"I beg pardon...?" Ella blinked. What in magic's name had just happened?

CHAPTER 18

THE SHOW GOES ON!

SUDDENLY ELLA KNEW EXACTLY HOW disoriented Harold must have felt. Fairweather continued walking back and forth in front of the large picture windows that overlooked the snow-covered town square outside.

Fairweather patted Ella's hand. "Are you feeling well? You look peaky. Perhaps a dose of my miraculous tonic will perk you up?" The matron dug around in her matching white lacy reticule. "Hold on, I keep a sample bottle in here... You'll like it. It's peppermint flavoured."

Ella extracted her limbs from the matron's grasp. She pursed her lips about to give the bad news and explain she hadn't been trying to offer the town hall ballroom as a replacement venue in which to hold *Lady MacDeath* when glancing around the vast space, the grand chandelier above, the stage, the chairs stacked waiting to cater to the citizens...

Come to think of it. This venue *would* make a fairly solid replacement for the playhouse theatre. "No need. I am perfectly well, I assure you."

Ella's thoughts returned to the opportunity presented. Fairweather had been alongside Bertram when he had been knocked over.

"But I was just thinking of the play's announcement. Indulge me, if you would, and cast your mind back to this morning when Bertram was unfortunately knocked over..."

Fairweather's sunny expression turned cloudy. "Not you too, your Ladyship! I shouldn't have thought *you* would hold water in that dreadful curse nonsense Beau was spouting."

Ella shook her head. "No, of course not."

"Thank goodness for that! He comes from terribly untrustworthy stock. Marley told me all about Beau's family." Fairweather bent forward, hand to heart in relief. "Gracious, when Beau came telling everyone about Spalding's near miss with the ropes backstage! Well! I tell you, even the seven secret herbs and spices in my patented tonic couldn't revive Nigella! She fainted clean away!"

"Ah..." Once again, Ella was at a loss for words. "I'm sorry, what happened?"

Fairweather harrumphed. "It was shortly after Bertram's accident. Spalding had run back inside. Do you remember?"

Ella nodded, yes she recalled Spalding running off when his father was knocked down. "Back into the 'deathtrap' of the building, as Bob said...."

"Yes, right. Beau followed after the boy—well, anyway, long story short. Beau came out later saying something about the boy being tangled in the ropes backstage—you know, the ones that lift the scenery? Apparently, the silly boy kicked a sandbag or something in anger, and the counterweight mechanism hoisted Spalding straight into the air!" Fairweather waved her hands in the air, miming panic. "Beau thought it was terribly funny! Going on about that nonsense curse. 'The father is knocked down and the son nearly hanged!' That's what Beau said, which I said was in terrible form..." Fairweather frowned. "But that's not what you were going to ask me about, was it?"

"Uh, no," Ella said, reeling at the peculiar events Fairweather had just detailed. Good gracious to think the son had had a near death experience just minutes following the tragic demise of his father!

The lines of the skipping song flit through her mind. *If I am trampled, who shall hang?*

She shook herself. Ridiculous! There was no curse! The good Doctor Hyde, however, had been accused of stealing Bertram's tie—that was a very real and dreadful incident which she needed to help clear up for her friend's sake. Not to mention Hyde wanted to find and test the tie for black magic residue. It really was important that it be found.

"Do you recall the red tie Bertram was wearing?" Ella asked the orphanage matron. "Did you perhaps remove it?"

Fairweather baulked, confused by the change of topic as Ella had been only minutes before. "The Ravensthorpe cravat? No, why?"

Ella was surprised. "You recognised the brand?"

Fairweather shrugged. "Certainly, Marley wears the same model of cravat. He recommended Ravensthorpe to me, you see. There was an eye-catching vibrant red tie on display most of last week when I was browsing. Come to think of it, I saw Spalding with a box from Ravensthorpe yesterday, before rehearsal. I wonder if he's the one who bought it...He said it was a gift."

Ella was intrigued. "A gift for his father? Was it the red tie?"

"I didn't see him open the box, I'm sorry. It could have been socks for all I know. You could ask Nigella, she was there. Why are you asking?"

Ella thought about what Hyde had told her. It wouldn't be wise to spread unfounded rumours of black magic, but she needed to come up with a plausible reason. "Hyde thought the cravat might have been caught in a wheel when Bertram fell and he needs the tie to conduct experiments and test his theory."

"Experiments? The doctor is a peculiar fellow. But if that's the case why not go ask Marley for an old one of his for Hyde's test? Or simply go and buy an identical version from Ravensthorpe's." She drew out a fancy ladies pocket watch from the lacy reticule. "I'm heading there myself in an hour, shopping for the children, if you want to come along."

"That is very kind of you, I would take that offer up. But I believe Hyde needs to test the original tie. Did you perhaps see anyone put it in a pocket for safekeeping?"

"Are you saying it's missing?" The matron looked appalled and fanned herself. "What would anyone want with a deadman's tie? That's very macabre." She shook herself. "I'm afraid I rather lost track of it after I wrestled Marley off of Bertram—poor chap lost his mind in the heat of the moment. Come to think of it..." The matron shook herself suddenly as if horrified by whatever she had been about to reveal. "Actually—no! That's ungracious of me to even think, Marley has been the epitome of chivalry in managing my new found fortune! He's got my vote! Or at least he had. I will vote for Nigella if she runs."

"Nigella?"

"Yes, poor duck has a bee in her bonnet over the closure of the theatre—she said just now she's thinking about running for mayor. Pop her hat in the ring, under a 'save the arts' platform. Once she's mayor she'll use her authority to restore the playhouse funding, or that's the plan. Naturally she asked me for the cash to whip the old death trap into shape—but there are limits! I'm already paying for the whole production!"

"You are?"

"It is to be my acting debut, and I want things done right!" The matron turned on the spot. "Speaking of, I must go bend Claude's ear again and beseech his better nature to accept my offer. I know that *boy*, Spalding, is Nigella's choice for male lead, but really! If I'm to launch my career *properly* then I need the *best* actor in town. I don't care if Claude's retired!" She thrust a large hand in her reticule and fumbled out the sample bottle of tonic, thumbed off the cork and swigged it down in one gulp. Wiping her lips on her sleeve, she wafted peppermint as she added, "I need a man, a real man like Claude at my side..." A hungry, glazed look came over the matron's expression, and she licked her lips, and thrust the empty tonic bottle in Ella's hand, demanding, "Do take care of this for me" before strutting out of the ballroom leaving a peppermint scented wake.

Ella squinted at the sample bottle labelled *Lily's Health Tonic* and had a cautious sniff of the bottleneck. She flinched. Of the seven secret herbs and spices, she rather suspected one was peppermint oil and the other six were gin.

CHAPTER 19

CAPTAIN WHO?

A FEW MINUTES LATER, AFTER placing the bottle in the ballroom kitchenette so it might be washed and reused, Ella exited the ballroom door and nearly smacked into Doctor Hyde who was entering.

"Ah, Mistress Charming! I'm glad I caught up with you again!" The doctor's worried expression made her draw up short. Now what? Was Bertram's widow Catherine impeding the good doctor's work?

"Doctor, you will be pleased to know I am making enquiries after the missing tie. I have spoken to Marley and Fairweather already, so there's just Nigella left. I will have your good name cleared in no time, I am sure. And once the tie is found you can conduct those *important* tests."

"I appreciate your concern for my reputation, but I suspect the widow's reaction was one of grief when she needed someone to blame. Grief affects people in strange ways. I have long come to terms with being the subject of people's frustration at the unfair departure of their loved ones..." Hyde removed his black felt hat and scratched his head. "But, yes, by all means, finding the tie is important if we hope to rule it out as the source of black magic that tainted Bertram's skin. However, it is of a far more important matter that I sought you out. Well, two important matters to be precise."

"Two?" Ella blanched. "By all means, I am all ears."

The doctor produced a newspaper cutting from his pocket on the article reporting Mr. Aladdin. "Marge was asking me a lot of peculiar questions following your visit this morning. Eventually she showed me this article... As soon as I finished speaking with Goldilocks about the unusual spate of accidental poisonings, I came to warn you and offer my deepest apologies. I cannot begin to express my horror!"

Ella nodded. "Thank you, I only became aware of Mr. Aladdin's outlandish statement recently myself. *We* are taking measures. There are certainly a lot of fortune hunter types wandering around town today..."

The doctor nodded. "Yes, and that is precisely my first matter of concern. There is a particular hunter I came to warn you about. I observed him outside the hospital and fortunately Marge knew his name..." The doctor turned to look over his shoulder as if fearful he might have been followed. "You may have heard of him, his reputation precedes him. He's a 'big game' hunter. Captain Ahab is his name."

"Captain Ahab...?" Ella narrowed her eyes. The name was unfamiliar to her. But if the doctor, who was usually so calm, was agitated, then something must be afoot.

"Whatever does this Captain Ahab look like?" Ella asked.

"The fellow only has one eye, the other is covered with a black eye patch."

For a second Ella thought the doctor was joking, but then she remembered who she was talking to as he continued.

"That's not all. His right leg was amputated at the knee and replaced with a pegleg."

Ella relaxed. "Oh dear, however will I spot him? Perhaps you had best tell me his hair colour as well?" Ella quipped, which earned her a sour face from the doctor.

"Mistress Charming, granted the gentleman in question would have to be a *master of disguise* to escape notice if you cross paths, but do not let your guard down. He had a tenacious air. My observation of his appearance indicates the chap is a professional who has *survived* being in the hunting game for a long while."

Ella conceded his point. Someone who had faced down tigers or lions would have no trouble capturing a domestic cat. "Very well, thank you for the warning. I shall keep a weather eye out for this Captain Ahab. But you said there was something else? Two important matters, you said."

"Yes. You recall I observed a spike in magical poisonings? And you suggested I speak to Goldilocks because she had mentioned a similar observation?"

Ella nodded.

"Miss Goldi informed me Charmington has a sophisticated magical wastewater system. A series of traps and such. She showed me one at the back of her Spa. Goldi explained that all waste liquids which have come in contact with magic must be deposited into these traps."

Ella nodded. "Yes, I had quite forgotten about the system. It was built as part of an upgrade to the infrastructure decades ago. To stop untreated magical wastewater being released into the rivers after the frog population began hallucinating they were princes. What of it?"

"Goldi suggested that perhaps there was a leak or damage along the pipe network. She indicated with the sudden increase in usage from last month's magical amnesty that the old system, having not been used in years, might have failed. Perhaps an overflow somewhere into drinking water?"

"Oh dear! That could certainly explain the poisonings you were seeing! We need to speak to Mr. Beau, he's the only one left on the maintenance staff. We will go ask Hansel, he might know where Mr. Beau is, I recall Hansel was going to arrange some keys for Mr. Beau to access a substation, whatever that is. We'll ask Hansel if he knows where we might find Mr. Beau. This way, please, doctor..."

———◆·—·—·——

LUCK APPEARED TO BE IN their favour, as while on their way through the town hall and connecting post office corridor Ella and the doctor bumped into Mr. Beau.

"Mr. Beau, a word if I may," Ella called, spotting the man in question at a narrow maintenance stairwell leading down to the basement levels. "You understand the working of the drains, am I correct?"

The shoeshine and gas lamp man flinched and looked around. "Haha! Caught me, red-handed!" he joked, throwing up his hands, as Ella and Doctor Hyde approached. "How may I be of service, marm?"

Ella let out a breath. "I was just informing Doctor Hyde that you are our resident expert in the plumbing systems."

Beau bowed before the doctor and the pair shook hands. "While I appreciate the title *expert*, it's only the gas system I'm qualified to be called an expert in. Like I told her ladyship before, my dad was the plumber, until his rival took the job out from under him. But whatever assistance I can offer, I am at your service."

"You're familiar with the wastewater traps system for magical residue?" Doctor Hyde asked, briefly going over what he had learned from Goldi.

Mr. Beau scratched his head. "A backwash of tainted magical wastewater? Hmm, the system is capable of handling a much higher capacity than what it received during last month's magic amnesty... though ice could be a factor. Assuming the traps themselves were blocked with ice, if they couldn't empty they *might* backflow out into the secondary water system that supplies the water fountains and ornamental features." He turned around on the spot. "I have to go check the East side substation anyways. The pressure values there will indicate if there's a problem..." He tapped his boot toe and looked perplexed. "And just when I thought fame and fortune awaited and I should be spending my afternoons troubled only by the signing of autographs and recounting the tale of poor Spalding swinging on high."

"Autographs?" Ella blinked. "I beg pardon?"

"On account of myself being related to one of the originals—the play-cursed four!" He waved a hand. "Nigella's announcement to hold *Lady MacDeath* as this year's Christmas production is the talk of the town. Four must die before opening night! Day's just started and we've had one killed already and a near miss when Spalding got caught in the scenery ropes and nearly hanged himself backstage. I was thinking of writing a memoir and living off of the sales."

Ella thinned her lips. "Isn't it rather glib? Your poor uncle was one of the original victims of the *Lady MacDeath* deaths."

"Yes indeed! Great old uncle Ebenezer—and that's what gives me a certain claim to fame now the curse has returned." He tutted. "Drowned in a bathtub, eh? What a fate. Of the cursed foursome it's the least admirable death."

"Surely you don't believe there's a genuine curse?" Ella asked. "The deaths preceding the opening night of the play all those years ago was an untimely coincidence, the leading lady being burned alive, and your uncle drowning in the bath. Tragic but perfectly mundane."

Beau swept his cap off his head and wrung it between his hands. "That may be, but you know theatre folk, they're a superstitious lot. Though when those ropes snaked about Spalding's neck—for a brief moment even I thought, *He's been hanged! The curse strikes again!* Nigella was there too, ask me if you don't believe me. And begging your pardon, marm, but given my current jobs I can't help but be jumpy. The Iron Drake shoe shine polish I use is part turpentine, plus what with me having to attend to the gas lamps—if ever any unlucky chap was likely to be burned to a crisp, it's gonna be me, ain't it?"

Frowning, Doctor Hyde chose to hold his silence, but Ella voiced disapproval at Mr. Beau's dark humour. "I cannot fathom why you find humour in the situation. Bertram was killed and if your account is to be believed, his son Spalding had a near miss. Your uncle's own passing may be nothing but the stuff of family legend to you, but this morning's events are a fresh tragedy to Bertram's family."

Beau leaned on one hip and lowered his voice in a conspiratorial fashion. "You know Bertram was also related to one of 'the originals', right? The leading lady whose dress caught fire on opening night was from his family, on his mother's side. They don't like to admit such now, considering what lofty heights the family has reached, but they had actresses and working class roots just a few generations back. And now, decades later, of all the people that could be knocked down and trampled, it's a descendant of the original four?" He slipped his cap back on his head. "So those that want to tempt fate I wish them good luck, but I for one will be *skipping* bath night this week!"

Ella held back another reprimand. Clearly the fellow wasn't interested in anything other than his own entertainment.

Mr. Beau gestured for the doctor to follow him, adding, "Now, good doctor, if you'd be so kind as to me follow me. It's a bit of a hike to the East side substation, so I think first we should do our due diligence and also check the valve room below the town hall. If there's nothing out of sorts here, we shall next inspect the substation pressure valves and find which of the wastewater traps is at fault. Good day, marm."

Hyde likewise bid Ella good day and set off with Mr. Beau to attend to the magical residue wastewater issue. Ella couldn't help frowning as Mr. Beau strolled away, whistling jauntily.

Really, how could the man be so jovial as to joke about the whole affair? Beau had a dark sense of humour. To joke about being burned alive? Magic preserve, that *would* be a truly dreadful way to die...

CHAPTER 20

NIGELLA REGRETS

ELLA SHOOK OFF HER MORBID thoughts. While the good doctor was doing his best to protect the town's water supply from any more magical or accidental poisonings, she would do her best to locate the missing red-tie so Hyde could test it for black magic. Marley and Fairweather hadn't been the only one at Bertram's accident, so too had Nigella. She might have loosened the tie and popped it in her pocket for safekeeping.

After collecting Tomcat from her tax office in the attic of the town hall—now cleverly disguised as Tomgoose—and asking around, Ella learned that despite Beau's warning, Nigella had just been seen venturing into the theatre...

Carrying Tomgoose bundled in her arms, his body wrapped in Sally's paisley scarf, and with a growing sense of trepidation, Ella crossed the threshold of the large, eerily quiet, playhouse once again.

Almost at once, Ella spied Nigella in the distance, at the foot of a staircase; her body language suggested the actress was contemplating her next move. Ella hung back. Whatever could Nigella up to? Lurking around in the darkened playhouse? No one should be here following the building being condemned this morning...

Keeping to the shadows and at a good distance behind, Ella stalked the other woman as Nigella lurched up stairs ahead, gripping the railing and wincing as she climbed. No doubt the actress's broken leg was not completely mended, and was giving her some discomfort.

It signalled Nigella's determination to be here...? Where was she going?

Since they were out of public sight, Ella set Tomcat—*Tomgoose*—down so he could walk unaided and they tracked the theatre company director to a row of doors up in the attic corridor. She picked one and disappeared from sight. Ella placed a finger to her lips, gesturing for Tom at her feet to be *extra* quiet.

The goose hat disguise bobbed sideways sharply, in a *you-don't-have-to-tell-me-twice* gesture.

Cautiously, Ella pressed up to the ajar door and peeped through the crack. Nigella was shuffling about a crowded, overfilled little box room. Was this prop storage? The room was filled with a collection of all manner of things, an overloaded clothes rack stuffed full of costumes, dresses in gaudy colours, purple silk, sparkly fabric with sequins that glittered like ice, another was covered in lace in reds and orange like flames. There was a fur-lined cloak in white next to a homely brown cloak in rough sacking material. A crowded table was covered in hat forms, wigs and men's cravats. The walls were plastered with posters advertising theatre productions going back decades.

Ella relaxed. Nigella wasn't lurking, she was picking through the items of her yesterdays. Lamenting the closure of this place that must have been her home for a long time.

A lump formed in Ella's throat and she regretted spying on the woman. Raising her knuckles she tapped lightly on the dressing door. "Nigella, it's me, Ella. Do you have a moment?"

"Come in," called the playhouse director. Inside Nigella was selecting items, picking them up, and placing them in a small battered leather suitcase which was balanced on a brass bedstead that looked to be a hundred years old. A hair brush. A bundle of stockings. A jewellery box. Nigella wasn't trying to hide anything, she was packing up her life.

"I didn't realise you were living here," Ella found herself saying, a flood of guilt and regret mixed in with the realisation. Why would Nigella be living here? Surely sleeping up in the playhouse attic must be uncomfortable. Cold, draughty, lonely... "Do you have somewhere to go?"

Nigella shrugged off the sadness in Ella's tone. "My sister runs an antique shop on the corner of Fifth and Main, it will do. She has cats. I'm allergic, but well...She finds me a bit...dramatic...so there you are." She let the implication hang, that neither of them would find the situation ideal, but family was family. Nigella took down a red silk petticoat hung over a line and Ella was reminded of her task for Doctor Hyde: find the red tie.

"I came because I need your help," Ella explained. "There's a bit of bother for Doctor Hyde, his professionalism has been questioned."

Nigella thrust her shoulders back. "The chap is a saint! Fixed my leg up a treat when others said I'd never walk again. Can you imagine!" She threw several paper fans into her suitcase.

"Yes, I quite agree. We are lucky to have such a doctor."

"Luck. Huh." Nigella grounded her teeth. "Uh! That wretched curse! The moment Spalding's father was bowled over, I realised my mistake. It's all my fault, you know. The seeds we sow and all that."

Ella blinked, disorientated by the actress' sudden mentioning of curses. "How so?"

"Money has been tight around here as you may have gathered from our need to bring on board a sponsor. None of the cast have been paid for months. I was really counting on this announcement. I thought, what a sensation it would cause! Putting on the cursed play! Who *wouldn't* come to watch me perform in *Lady MacDeath*?" She stuffed an item in the case, strapped the lid closed and tested the weight. "And now we're shut down. No one will see us perform. That's how I'm to blame."

"No one blames you," Ella said stoically. "It was just bad timing."

"Yes, well bad timing makes people point fingers. You know as well as I, *everyone* wants *someone* to blame."

Quite so. Ella nodded. "Speaking of, as I said. I'm trying to track down what happened to the red tie Bertram was wearing this morning when he was knocked down. It's gone missing and the family is upset. Did you see someone remove it, to help Bertram breathe? Maybe pop it in their pocket?"

"Not that I saw," Nigella said with a sigh, "but I know the one you mean, assuming we're both thinking of the scarlet cravat gifted to Spalding."

"Wait, I'm sorry. Are you saying the tie Bertram was wearing actually belonged to his son Spalding?"

The actress shrugged. "You'll have to ask Spalding, but he told me an anonymous fan had dropped it off yesterday. He opened the box while in my presence last night and showed me. The box was left in his dressing room. Unsigned, but there was an encouraging note, urging Spalding to stick to '*what he's good at rather than following in his father's footsteps*.' It's no secret Spalding's father wants–er, *wanted* Spalding to follow in his footsteps and leave the theatre for politics." Nigella dusted her hands. "But well, when I saw it about Bertram's neck this morning I guessed that Spalding decided to 're-gift it' as the young ones say. I didn't blame him, as I said before, we're all rather short on funds..." She sighed. "I am fortune's fool. I should not have broken the code of the theatre. I evoked the curse upon us all by mocking the theatre gods..."

Ella could only nod. No one liked to be mocked.

"It's sad really," Nigella muttered, picking through a collection of wigs and placing one gently into the suitcase, "they were rivals in their youth too. Beau told me all about it. Marley and Bertram were in love with the same girl, but Marley came from lowly roots, he didn't know who his father was and his mother was a laundress, who worked for one of the schools of magic, Harvey's or Harrisons, something like that."

"Haversham?"

"Yes! That was it."

Ella narrowed her eyes. Marley's mother worked as the laundress at Haversham academy where Ella herself had studied magic? Oh good gracious! A thought occurred. Though she had been unable to locate the red tie, perhaps the box it came in might shed some light? Hyde could have the box tested for black magic residue. She gripped Nigella's elbow. "Would the wastepaper basket in Spalding's dressing room have been emptied? I'd like to see the tie's packaging for myself."

"Why? Is the box important?" Nigella answered, looking concerned, "I imagine it's still there, but Spalding's dressing room is down below the stage. Where Beau reported the gas leak is..."

Chapter 21

The Ravensthorpe Clue

Ella paused. "Did you hear that?" she whispered, looking back over her shoulder.

"What?" asked Tomcat, his goose-head disguise tipping sideways.

"A scraping noise, kind of tap, *drag*, tap, *drag*. The sound a one-legged character might make while trying to discreetly follow after someone."

Tomcat's paws clamped to the side of the goose-head hat. "Can you release the strap? I can't hear so well with this on."

She did so and Tomcat's pointy white triangle ears twitched as he listened. After a minute his whiskers fanned and he raised his little nose to sniff the air. "There's nothing I can hear or scent."

Relieved, Ella shook off the notion they were being watched. "I could well have imagined it. I am jumping at shadows after what Hyde said about that big game hunter chap, Ahab."

Tomcat tapped a paw to his chin. "By the way, does the gas they use to light the street lamps have an odour? Mr. Beau said the theatre is filling up with a gas leak, right? That's why it's been shut down. But I can't smell anything."

"I confess I don't know if the streetlamp gas has an odour. The lamps were installed after I began living out in the woods." Ella shrugged. "But gas is heavier than air, it *sinks*, I know that much. And the stage here isn't at the bottom of the theatre, there's a basement below. That's where the gas will be pooling."

Tomcat nodded. "That makes sense, I guess." Free from the constraints of his goose costume he stretched and padded ahead through a door labelled *dressing room*.

Ella picked up the goose-head hat and followed. He was already peering into the wastepaper basket, a paw clamped to his nose when Ella entered a second behind. "I can definitely smell black magic," Tomcat uttered, peering into the bin where a red Ravensthorpe box was nestled among lunch wrappers and newspapers. "Don't touch it with your bare hands!" he cautioned when Ella went to remove the box from the basket. "Put on those gloves Goldi gave you."

"A very good point," Ella said, freeing the white sparkly gloves from her pocket and slipping them on. For a second her hands thrummed and she wondered how many times she could use them before their protective enchantment faded. She hadn't forgotten they still planned to venture out to Haversham's library in search of a book or article that might reveal what would happen to Tom's memories when he was restored to his human form.

Ella placed the Ravensthorpe box on the dressing table and Tomcat leapt up beside it, careful not to touch the box as Ella gently opened it. There was nothing visually untoward. The exterior was embossed with the words Ravensthorpe while the inside of the box was lined with black silk. Overall it appeared of high quality.

"Ugh." Tom's paw returned to his nose. "I can't *see* anything, but the scent is vivid—it's not like other times I have come across black magic." His whiskers curled in distaste and ears flattened to his head. "I think this black magic spell is *fresh*."

Ella and Tom exchanged worried glances. In the past months most of the black magic they had come across was from old items, a film of residue built up and dulled by time, but still enough to corrupt minds with constant contact.

"Fresh and *strong*," Tom gagged, backing away. "Can't you sense it?"

Ella shook her head. "I assume it's a side effect of my magical powers being bound. The box appears perfectly ordinary to me, as it would any human. But I trust your sensitivity to black magic."

Ella closed the box, and held it in one palm while using her other hand she peeled off the glove holding the box and wrapped it to enclose it within the glove.

"Better?"

Tom nodded, his shoulders sagging. "Much, thank you."

Ella sighed. They would have to seek Goldi's help to dispose of this item, perhaps using the wastewater trap—but no, that was for magical waste liquids.

Tom peered over the edge of the table down at the paper bin. "What about the note? Is that in there too?"

Grimacing, Ella fossicked around in the trash one-handed. Under some orange peels she extracted a cream card, and handwritten in blue fountain pen ink the words exactly as Nigella had described, *Stick to what you're good at.*

"But unsigned."

"There might have been an outer paper wrapper." Tom encouraged. "Look again."

"What were you saying before about the *joys* of having thumbs?" Ella asked as she tipped the basket out.

Tom chuckled. "As soon as I'm restored to a human being again, I will gladly handle all the filthy tasks. You have my word. You can go back to being a princess, spending all your time ordering me about. Tom, cut the wood. Tom, light the fire. Tom, polish my boots. Read me a bedtime story and make sure to do the voices."

"Hmm," Ella muttered as she rifled through receipts, apple cores and other rubbish, placing them one by one back into the bin. Her life had changed so much for the better since Tom had entered her garden all those months ago. Forcing her to mingle again with the general Charmington population. To get involved in the community. What would life be like once he left? A return to loneliness?

"There's nothing," Ella concluded at last when she had returned all the contents back into the wastepaper basket.

She stood. "So, let's assume, Spalding finds the box and note here on his dressing table. He concludes it's a gift from an admirer."

Tomcat green eyes narrowed, as if imagining the scenario. "I agree. That sounds plausible."

"But the tie—assuming it was the red tie inside—which we can't prove until we find the wretched thing. But assuming it was tie, enchanted with black magic—"

"That Hangman's Knot spell you told Hyde about."

"Yes, enchanted with the Hangman's Knot spell. And once tied around the wearer's neck, it tightens and tightens until they asphyxiate." Ella held up two fingers. "Two problems with that theory."

"Spalding has no enemies, and why didn't he try the tie on?" Tomcat said, putting voice to Ella's thoughts.

"Yes. Why didn't Spalding try on the tie?" She paced about the little room. "It's human nature. When you are given something. A tie, a ring, a necklace. You *try* it on."

"That hangman's spell. Can it be, er, *activated* only when it comes into contact with its intended victim? What if Spalding wasn't the target? What if the person who gave it to him knew he was going to give it to his dad?"

Ella dismissed the idea. "No. The Hangman's Knot spell's beauty is in its simplicity. *Whoever* puts it on will suffer the effects. As soon as the knot is tied it starts to tighten."

"How do you know this kind of creepy stuff?"

"Didn't I ever tell you, I came top of my class in black magic? No? Anyways, so for whatever reason, Spalding opens the box but doesn't put the tie on. Most likely another person came into the room—ah! Of course Nigella was there. So back to our theory. What does this tell us?"

"Spalding has an enemy we know nothing about?"

Ella nodded. "Quite so...Spalding has a secret enemy."

CHAPTER 22

GEESE ARE ALL THE RAGE

"SINCE WE CAN'T SEEM TO trace what happened to the tie or who has it now, but because the box we believe it came in does have the taint of black magic..." Ella said, her gaze lingering on the empty tie box now wrapped in the single glove. "Our investigation leads us to answer, *who* left the necktie in Spalding's dressing room?"

Tomcat's ears stood up. "Where do we start?"

"We start at Ravensthorpe tailor's shop. See if they can tell us who purchased it."

Tom narrowed his eyes. "Does Ravensthorpe dabble in black magic?"

Ella shook her head. "I doubt that very much. Such a scandal could ruin them. We will have to be careful with what we say if I want them to answer my questions. But what I suspect is, someone placed a black magic curse on the tie *after* they bought it."

Tom nodded thoughtfully. "That makes sense."

Ella dusted off her hands. "Right, let's pop that goose-hat disguise on you and we'll see if you can pass for a believable goose out in public."

Tom lifted his chin proudly. "I have been practising making goose noises—would you like to hear?"

Ella adjusted the strap. "No, Tom."

THE DOORMAN SALUTED AND OPENED the door for Ella. "Thank you, very kind," she acknowledged with a regal nod as she stepped over the threshold. Tomcat was secure in her arms, his goose-head disguise strapped on tightly, his small, fluffy body swaddled in her paisley shawl.

The doorbell was still tinkling as Ella entered. The scent of polished wood, pressed linen, and faintly spiced cologne greeted them while a thin waif of a girl in a smart black frock approached. "Good day, your ladyship," the shopgirl said with a curtsey. "Welcome to Ravensthorpe Tailors. My name is Maisy... Er..." The girl's routine greeting faded on her lips as she registered the bulk of what appeared to be a large white goose in Ella's arms, staring back at her with a glassy-eyed stare.

Ella patted the goosehat disguise covering Tomcat. "Geese are all the rage in Avalon," she explained, a little haughtily, nose in the air. "My brother, Merlin, has two."

The young sales clerk, Maisy, pressed her lips together, doing her best to suppress the *rich-people-be-crazy* expression on youthful features. Ella turned away, pretending not to notice, and perused the men's display of cravats and silk handkerchiefs.

The young saleswoman assumed a respectful distance nearby, close enough to be at Ella's beck and call, but not so close as to invite familiarity.

Ella turned on her heel sharply. "These cravats," she mused, trailing her fingers over a selection of silks. "An acquaintance recently purchased a striking red one from here. I forget his name. I want one, just like it. Do you know the item I mean?"

Maisy half-bowed. "One moment, your ladyship. I will check the register..."

Ella waved a languid hand, indicating, *Very well, run along.* After a few minutes of browsing the umbrella, hats and socks, a polite cough drew Ella over to the mahogany and glass counter where the sales assistant had a leather sales ledger open.

"The only red one was purchased a few days ago. We don't have any more in stock, but I can order you one in."

"How can you be *sure* it's the same?" Ella snipped.

"Ah, well, we record down the colour and make, for stocktaking. There was only one gentleman's cravat in scarlet."

"Be a dear, Maisy, and tell an old woman who bought it?" Ella changed up her tone, and smiled pleasantly. "Then I'll be sure."

"Certainly." The young woman tapped the account book. "It was purchased on credit and put on Jacob Marley's account."

Marley... Spalding's father's political rival. The only real contender to go up against Bertram. "And you're sure? Marley bought it?"

The girl blinked. "Sure as I can be, your ladyship. Penelope serviced the counter that day. See, this is her signature. I'm afraid she quit work this morning, but Penny wouldn't let just anyone place an item on credit. She would have known exactly who she was speaking to."

"Hmm… I see." Ella let out a breath and leaned against the counter, letting it take part of Tom's weight.

So Marley *did* purchase the tie? The question remained, why had Marley posed as an *anonymous* fan and given the tie to Spalding?

"Um… Shall I order one for you, your ladyship?" The shop assistant's gaze kept straying to the goose.

If it hadn't been for Hansel's dire warning about the state of the kingdom's finances, Ella would have glibly put half a dozen expensive ties on Sibylla's account. But as things stood, Sibylla would simply refuse to pay and the poor girl would wind up having her wages docked. Ella shook her head. "I think not…let me think on it, my dear… But you have been most helpful."

"Forgive me, your ladyship. But with your brother being Merlin, the famous magician, do you know about magic and stuff…?" The shop girl, wide-eyed, leaned closer to Ella and whispered. "Is it true what they're saying? About the *Lady MacDeath* curse?"

Ella narrowed her eyes. In the crook of her arm, Tom's goose-head dipped sideways in a questioning manner. "What are they saying?"

"That young Mr. Spalding accidentally invoked the curse. Brought it down on his own family." The shopgirl looked left and right, her wide eyes returned to stare at the supposed goose in Ella's arms. "Mr. Beau told me he heard the actor evoke it. *Three must die before opening night!* Mr. Spalding's very words. And then his own father goes and gets runs down, and minutes later Spalding is strangled by a stage rope—just like that skipping rhyme. *One is trampled, two is hanged.*" She shuddered. "Gives me the right shivers!"

Ella thought over this new information and compared it to her recollection of Bertram's death. Both Bertram's own son Spalding, and his political rival, Marley were there, arguing with him about their futures shortly after Nigella had announced the cursed play.

It was true that Spalding himself had been first to voice that to break the curse three must die before opening night…

Could the lad have been 'acting' distressed?

Ella shook her head. No, that reasoning was flawed. Overly complicated. Marley was right there, he had means, he had motive, and he had an opportunity.

She had seen his hands clutched about Bertram's throat, shaking the man and shouting, '*You awful old codfish!*'

The only question that remained was, did an enraged Marley pull the tie tight and throttle Bertram? Or, had he indeed placed a black magic spell on the tie, and merely taken advantage of the moment to watch the life squeezed from his rival?

In her mind's eye, she remembered Marley picking up the fallen top hat of his rival, and dusting it off. That strange look of disgust and yet satisfaction crossed his face.

The face of a murderer?

It would be prudent to double-check that it was in fact Marley who had purchased the tie. That would confirm her growing theory that he was responsible for the black magic spell.

"Maisy, my dear. Can you please tell me where your colleague Penny lives?"

"Certainly, that's easy. She's quit work here to go be Mr. Marley's housekeeper. I told you, Penny would have known who she was serving." She smiled brightly. "Shall I write down the address for you?"

"You are most kind, my dear." Ella nodded and turned away to browse the shop window display while she waited. But on glancing out across the street a figure made her gasp and clutch Tom tightly.

Under the lamppost, Harold Harper stood conversing to a one-eyed man with a black eye-patch and a pegleg. Certainly that must be the notorious Captain Ahab, the big game hunter that Doctor Hyde had wanted her of. Judging from the hand-waving and pointing, Harold was giving directions. The pair shook hands, a smug grin of satisfaction spreading across Harold's face and then they both crossed the street, heading directly for Ravensthorpe tailors!

Magic preserve! Could that toad Harold be collaborating with the captain to capture Tomcat?

Ella spun around and snatched up the address. "Thank you, my dear, I shall head there directly! One last request—does this shop have a backdoor?"

CHAPTER 23

HAVERSHAM'S LIBRARY

"WHY ARE WE IN THIS neighbourhood?" Tomcat questioned, his goosehat bobbing left and right as if he had trouble seeing, as Ella's hobnail boots crunched the fresh snow fallen on the winter-stripped tree lining East Avenue. "When you told the shopgirl we were going straight to Marley's house?"

Ella let out a long breath. "Because I have no doubt Maisy will pass on that precise location to Harold and that game hunter, Captain Ahab. We'd be best to avoid him, I feel. Besides, have you forgotten? We needed to use Haversham's library to research what might happen to your memories if Goldi prematurely nudges your essence back into your human body..." She looked over her shoulder then darted down the path leading to the side entrance of the abandoned Haversham Academy.

The side door hung ajar.

"Oh, dear, never a good sign," Ella muttered, setting the supposed goose down at her feet.

Tomcat shucked off the hat disguise as she hooked the door open with the handle of her walking stick and they peered inside the entrance area. What had formerly been dusty now showed recent signs of life. Several sets of muddy footprints tracked in. All the watercolours paintings that had hung on the foyer walls were gone. Only the white cloths that had covered the paintings were left, pooled on the marble floor.

Tomcat's ears twitched as he tipped his head, this way and that, using his superior animal hearing. "I can't hear anything, but it's a big building. If people are living here now, I can't detect anyone inside at the moment."

Ella sucked a breath between her teeth and tapped the walking stick sharply on the hard tiles, twice. The double-tap engaged the light function and a soft glow stretched out. "I doubt anyone would be squatting here, the neighbours would have noticed and reported it. But certainly, with the magical amnesty last month, I'm sure people suffering hard times might have been desperate enough to break in to see what valuables or magical items were left to take and sell." Together they ventured inside.

Ella's thoughts seemed to ring true. Paintings and vases were missing from plinths. Someone had attempted to take the heavy old grandfather clock. It was on its side in the main corridor.

She spared it barely a glance and orientated herself to her memories of having studied in this school many decades ago. "The library is up this staircase, on the next level. Hopefully the magical books collection hasn't been pilfered. I imagine there would be limited resale value for such contraband, at least locally..."

"I've been thinking," Tom said, as both their feet scuffed whispery sounds in the plush Persian carpet as they climbed the grand staircase. "In case I lose my memory of the past five months, once I become human again, I should write myself a letter. You know, explain all the things I've done."

"That's a good idea," Ella agreed, "although as I will have to write the letter for you, since your paws can't hold a pen, do you think you'd trust a letter supposedly of your thoughts, but written in my handwriting? You didn't know me when you swapped bodies with my cat after you accidentally wished on a star. If I remember correctly, you thought I had turned you into a cat, because I was an evil witch..."

"Oh gosh! I'd forgotten I blamed you for that," Tom said, sounding embarrassed, as Ella gestured to the twin wooden doors on the landing.

"You could ask Cassidy to write the letter—you knew and trusted her before you became a cat."

"But I can hardly ask Cassidy to write a letter to preserve my memory of how much more I like her now!"

Ella held her tongue. She didn't blame Tom's outburst. The poor lad was in a truly tricky spot.

"Here's the library..." She grasped a brass handle and they peered in the hushed room. Inside the air was thick and dusty. All the windows were shuttered, except for one. The shutters had been folded back and the bookcase nearest the window had books strewn about on the carpet.

They padded over to the disturbance.

"Domestic spells," Tomcat said, choosing one of the fallen books and reading the title. He squinted at the subtitle. "*A Magical Guide to Maintaining a Healthy and Happy Home*." He nudged another title aside. "*Sixty Spells for stubborn stains...*" He blinked. "These don't sound dangerous. They sound useful."

"It's not always the spell that's dangerous. It's the intention of the user..." Ella's eyes alighted on one thin red book which lay further away, directly under the unshuttered windowsill, as if someone had taken it over to the light to study it better. The book's pages were fanned open. Ragged white paper edges within revealed pages had been ripped out. She bent down and picked it up and read the journal label, *The Old Sailor's Guide to Knots: useful rope tricks for Business and Buildings from Barns to Windmills.*

"For example," Ella muttered, "a spell to ensure a knot doesn't slip seems harmless enough when it's used on a rope to secure a load or hold fast a windmill arm..."

She flicked through to the back index. Traced her fingertip down the letter H. *Hangman's nooses and knots* were listed. Ella then hunted through the pages, searching for the page number listed and the corresponding missing pages confirmed her suspicion. "Yes... Someone has ripped out a version of the Hangman's Knot spell from this book..."

"Did you really cast black magic spells back in the day?" Tomcat uttered. "I know I accused you of being a mean witch back when we first met, and I know now there are different kinds of witches, but I can't imagine you having anything to do with black magic."

"I was top of academic black magic *theory*," Ella explained grimly. "Unlike my brilliant twin sister, I had little natural wyld magic. I was the family dunce. Academic magic was my ticket to self respect and advancement, or so I thought... Theory of magical study is—*was*— open to anyone, regardless of whether their wyld magic was strong, weak, or non-existent. And Mrs. Haversham was so...enchanting. So accomplished and intelligent. When she encouraged me to study the dark arts I was flattered. I had never had anyone take an interest in *my* potential, but..."

Tomcat's green eyes blinked in the library shadows. "But...?"

"But after I excelled in theoretical study, she wanted me to take the next step, advance on to *practical* applications. I didn't realise at the time, she wanted me to become like her... Become a full blown practitioner of black magic."

Tomcat clamped a horrified paw across his mouth. "What did she do? Threaten you?"

Ella snorted. "She had no need to threaten me. I was putty in her hands! I hung on every word of praise she ladled upon me!"

Tomcat gulped. "What...happened?" He reached out, put a paw to Ella's knee. "You're a good person, Ella. You care about everyone. You would never hurt anyone! Surely Haversham should have known that?"

"I am sure, *if* she had come to me—twirling a black moustache—and said, 'Black magic's reputation is entirely undeserved-*mwahahaha!*' I would have been suspicious. But the truth is, I *didn't* know the first spells she presented to me *were* black magic."

"But how? How could you not know?"

Ella sighed. "You see, a nasty measles-like illness started going around the local human children. These awful red spots appeared. They cried all night. They were in such pain... Haversham told me of a remarkable healing spell. But it was meant for adults, not children, and least of all fragile children. She said we would need to tinker with the spell. And then, test it... I remember she showed me this little white mouse. Oh, it was so sweet. A little pink nose and whiskers." Ella gulped as tears sprang to her eyes. "'*How can you quibble to sacrifice one vile rodent if it will save many human babies? Their mothers will thank you,*' she said. '*They will owe you their children's lives... Their human children's lives.*'"

Ella wiped her sleeves across her eyes and peered out the window. Once she had stood in this library, studying these books, she had opened this very window wide, lifted the sash as a young woman called up to her, holding aloft her happy and healthy toddler...

"And they did, you know, thank me. Everywhere I went, proud mothers would stop and show their babies. *Thank you, Mistress Ella!* I remember one father, he owned the tailor shop in the arcade, he made me a fine cloak, and another, a composer, wrote a piece of music. Several families named their next born after me! Can you imagine?" Ella turned away from the window. "I had never felt anything like it. So much praise. So much gratitude. My vanity was well fed I can tell you. Exactly as Haversham hoped it would be."

Tomcat gulped again. "But you told me once that Haversham hated humans. Why would she help them?"

"It was only much, much later with the knowledge of hindsight that I recognised her hatred. I'm not proud of how long it took me to come to that conclusion." She raised her eyes to Tom's. "When Mrs. Haversham gave me the white mouse, her intention wasn't to *teach* me a black magic spell, her intention was to *test* me. To see if I would *sacrifice* the mouse—to see if I might align with her thinking that *some lives* are expendable, less worthy..." Ella crushed the memory. How foolish she had been. How blind. To Haversham all human lives were worth less. "Can't you guess where the measles epidemic came from in the first place?"

Tomcat's white fur stood on end. "You're not saying that she—that Haversham—was involved?"

Ella let out a weary sigh. "That's exactly what I'm saying. The whole epidemic was a set up. Haversham herself had started the measles epidemic so she could test whether I might be a compliant apprentice..." She gave herself a mental shake. "Now, where were we?"

Ella bent down and rifled through the other books on the carpet. "Even a domestic spell is dangerous in the wrong hands, or done with ill intentions." She picked up a book and showed Tom the title: *Long Lasting Laundry Spells for Gentlemen on the Go*, and *How to ensure smart Appearances in Public*. "Like combining a Hangman's Knot with a laundry spell."

"A lethal combination."

"Agreed. So, let's review. What do we know? Bertram's death, which at first appears to be a tragic accident—"

"Or the first death in a notorious local playhouse curse," Tom interjected.

Ella placed her hands on her hips. "I don't believe the 'curse' of the *Lady MacDeath* play! Plays don't curse people. People curse people..."

Tomcat's ears dipped. "And I'm just saying! Just because *you* don't believe in it, doesn't mean someone else doesn't!"

Ella scowled. "False curses to one side, Doctor Hyde concludes that the death of Bertram is due to asphyxiation, not due to being struck down—which was the supposed *Lady MacDeath* curse's detail. And furthermore, Bertram has black magic residue in his blood. Unfortunately, the red cravat the deceased was wearing has been misplaced, so it can't be tested."

Tomcat's hackles raised. "With you so far. Go on."

"A gift of some item of men's apparel—which we assume was the red cravat Bertram was wearing—from Ravensthorpe—the box of which you confirmed *was* tainted with black magic residue—is delivered to the young actor Spalding the day before, as witnessed by

Nigella. Not only that, but the recipient of the gift, Spalding, is the son of Bertram, who wanted his son to join him in politics, and the gift also included an unsigned note encouraging Spalding to *'stick to what he's good at.'* Which we must assume is acting, although I've never seen Spalding perform, so we'll take that one with a proverbial grain of salt."

Tom rubbed his chin thoughtfully. "And Marley is the political rival of Bertram..."

"Quite so. Next, you and I confirmed that a red cravat was purchased from Ravensthorpe and put on Marley's account this week, and lastly..." Ella held up the sailor's journal and one of the domestic laundry spell books. "Nigella reminded me that Marley's mother was a laundress who worked right here at the Haversham academy back in the day. So, do we agree on the murder weapon and killer?"

"I think so..." Tomcat nodded. "Okay, so our theory is that the red cravat purchased from Ravensthorpe was enchanted with a Hangman's Knot laundry spell, and used as the murder weapon which killed Bertram..."

Ella took up the summary, "Yes. Even though his son, Spalding was probably the intended target, the end goal was to get Bertram out of the running for mayor, and therefore the guilty party is...?"

Tomcat nodded and met her eyes, as one they both said, "Marley."

"One hundred percent."

"Undoubtedly... I must say, I really feel I have the hang of this sleuthing lark." Ella slotted the books back into the bookcase and dusted her hands. "Oh bother! I forgot to put on those protective gloves Goldi gave me!"

CHAPTER 24

BURNED UP

ELLA STOOD BACK FROM THE library shelves to better survey the rows of book titles. "Now, let's focus on *your* predicament. Shall we hunt first for books about transformation, or something on memories?"

Tomcat blinked. "Huh? Why? Shouldn't we go to confront Marley? Doctor Hyde is depending on our help."

"True, but I promised you at the start of today that we'd find how to return you to your human form so you can talk to Cassidy—as an equal—before she leaves. I intend to keep that promise! But Goldi was also worried that returning you to your human body abruptly *might* eradicate your memories of the last five months. And here we are, in the best magical library in town! The answer must lie in one of these many, many books. The clock is ticking! You told me that Cassidy leaves tomorrow."

Tomcat hunched and his tail flicked. "I know you promised, and I'm grateful. But even if I could become human tonight with my memories intact, I wouldn't try and stop Cassidy from leaving. It would be unfair and selfish. If you love something, let it go."

Ella drew breath to argue, but then stopped herself. *If you love something, hold it tight and lock it up*, did sound a touch...evil. She fanned herself with her hands. "It's rather stuffy here. I think the black magic residue is affecting my sinuses."

Tomcat tipped his head sideways. "I don't think there is any black magic residue in here, I feel perfectly well."

"Agree to disagree, but since you're not keen on resolving your love-life problems just yet, let's track down Marley before he burns the wretched tie and we lose our evidence," Ella said, turning on her heel with a swish of her long black skirts. "Come along. Let's pop your goose hat back on..."

The pair set off, Ella bundling Tom 'goose' up in her arms.

Outside the wind had picked up, snow flurries swirled around. Ella cast a furrowed brow at the darkening sky and drew her scarf across her face. Hunched into the wind she and Tom were able to carry on with their conversation as they trekked north.

"How will we get past Captain Ahab, if he is camped outside Marley's house?" Tom muttered. "Shall I run past and see if he will chase me?"

Ella mulled the idea over. "A bit risky, but it might work. I was also thinking we should fetch Robinne's help. It would be foolish of me to put us both in danger by confronting him alone—if Marley hasn't disposed of the tie, the fabric might well contain enough black magic to perform the Hangman's knot spell several more times, depending how strong the saturation was and the laundering methods."

"That's good thinking. Although maybe we should better ask Cassidy to back us up? Not because I want to see her as much as possible before she leaves—in case you were thinking that. But because she's a professional town guard."

Ella bit back a retort. She had been thinking exactly that, but no matter. "I will grab the first trustworthy and able-bodied acquaintance whose path we cross. How about that?"

Tomcat's goose head hat suddenly jerked. "Ella! Can you hear that? Bells! Something is on fire!"

Ella pushed back her cloak hood and looked up to the skyline above the stone buildings. A haze of smoke curled skyward, black against the wintry dusk, carrying the acrid scent of scorched paper.

A person running by called out, "The town hall is on fire!"

Tomcat immediately leapt from Ella's arms, and cursing under her breath, Ella ran after his bizarre form—a goose with four legs and a tail!

A fire in the town hall was the last thing the kingdom's dwindling finances needed—how would they ever find funds for a hefty repair bill to one of the grandest, and most necessary buildings in town? Thank goodness the town hall had sprinklers! Whatever damage should be limited and hopefully no one would be injured or killed!

THE NARROW SIDE STREETS OFF Northgate Square, where Mercer Lane intersected with the various town hall buildings thrummed with urgency as the town cluckoo clock tolled its clamorous warning. The cobbles were slick with snow trampled underfoot by townsfolk rushing here and there.

Shouts rang out over the din—calls for water, orders barked by the town guards, the panicked wails of onlookers clutching handkerchiefs to their mouths. A bucket chain of the able-bodied snaked from the town hall alleyway off to presumably the nearest well, Ella surmised by the passing of sloshing buckets hand to hand with desperate speed.

"But what of the sprinklers?" Hadn't Mr. Beau reported that very morning the town hall itself was in relatively good repair—could he have been mistaken? Or had another pipe burst?

Through the chaos, Ella wove her way forward, dodging careening townsfolk and the occasional upended bucket of icy water. Above the tumult, the imperious voice of Mistress Fairweather rose like a brass bell, herding a gaggle of orphans into the fray—not to help, but to hand out tiny green bottles of her 'restorative patented tonic' to any frazzled bystander willing to take one.

"Health tonic! Mistress Fairweather's own special remedy!" a curly-haired boy called, waving a bottle aloft.

The Baker Street orphans, usually dressed in homely but durable yellow and blue striped jumpers and corduroy knickerbockers, were nearly unrecognizable in their absurdly fine garb—rich velvets, silk sashes, gleaming brass buttons ill-suited to the soot-streaked, frantic streets. They scurried like well-trained mice, clutching sample bottles to distribute, their voices adding to the chaos.

Ella's stomach twisted as she craned her neck, her gaze locking onto a broken office window. "Marley's office," she whispered. No? Yes! Magic preserve! She had been inside that very room not a month prior. Now, the stonework above the broken window was stained black with smoke, and all about the air rained fragments of paper and ash.

The clock tower bells suddenly stopped their relentless chime and there was a relaxation among those standing in the bucket chain as word passed the fire was doused. Buckets were set at feet, as people wiped their brows and loosened collars, but no one broke the line in case the order was reversed.

The air swirled with flakes of ash and snow as Mistress Fairweather bustled through the townsfolk like a galleon in full sail, her broad skirts sweeping aside cinders and knocking over pails with each imperious step. Her sharp eyes darted about, not in concern for the fire, but for the well-being of her charges—and, more importantly, their impeccable attire.

Fairweather, beaming with pride, directed her miniature army with the air of a woman bestowing great charity upon the suffering masses. "Mind your clothes—no soot, no spills! Run along and play now children. I'll take over." She yanked the collar of a child who had strayed dangerously close to a puddle of ash-streaked water, before adding her own voice to the sales pitch, "Drink up, drink up! The glacial spring water and secret ingredients soothes the nerves!"

Ella watched the scene with a mixture of exasperation, suspecting as she did the 'secret ingredient' was likely gin, and judging by the gagging reflexes of those flush-cheeked few who were sampling it, the tonic was more likely to reignite flames than settle nerves.

A new stir passed through the crowd and people nearest the side entrance stood back as Cassidy, dressed in her guards uniform, emerged from the doorway, followed closely by Spalding and Mr. Beau. Between them, they carried a stretcher, a limp body covered by a cloth. The gathered townsfolk hushed momentarily as they passed.

But then a skipping chant rang through the air, one of the orphans singing,

> *If one is trampled, who shall hang?*
> *Drown them in the bathtub, and what's more,*
> *Water in your lungs is hard to survive.*
> *Hear the lady screaming, burning alive!*

"Hush, children! Hush!" Fairweather scolded as Spalding's gaze flickered toward the children, his jaw tightening.

His face was pale, his hands clenched about the stretcher handles. Poor lad, to think his own father had died that very morning in equally bizarre and tragic circumstances…

An unease curled in Ella's gut. Two deaths in one day, and come to think of it, Spalding—and Mr. Beau—were present for both.

Ella's breath stilled. The deaths described in that rhyme were starting to feel eerily familiar. No! That was a ridiculous notion. There was no *Lady MacDeath* curse, it was superstitious playhouse nonsense! A coincidence!

Shaking off the doubt, Ella approached Cassidy who was with a senior town guardsman, tending to the bucket-line of citizens, passing the official word they were no longer needed, and taking time to thank each who came out to assist. The words "Marley" and "Suicide" quickly became repeated.

Ella was startled. "What?" She grabbed Cassidy's arm and pulled the young guardswoman aside. "Repeat that if you please?"

"There was no note," Cassidy replied, keeping her voice low. "But there was a bottle of poison found beside Mr. Marley. He had an empty glass in his hand."

A sharp, disbelieving gasp cut behind Ella.

"No! No, no!" Mistress Fairweather bustled forward, pink-cheeked with indignation. "He was in perfectly good spirits when he was going over my new fortune earlier today! The mayoral race was Marley's for the taking! I won't have you besmirch my accountant's good name!"

Ella raised an eyebrow. "Are you sure he was fine? People don't always—"

"Yes! We went over his acceptance speech this morning—what more proof do you need?" She jabbed a finger at Cassidy and Ella both. "Why didn't the sprinklers come on?! Who is responsible for their upkeep? I pay my taxes! Where is Mr. Beau?" She picked up her skirts and turned away, indignation vibrating off her, sending ash and snowflakes shimmering off the ostrich feathers of her gaudy bonnet. "This is an outrage! Children, attend me! Where is our carriage? Who remembers where we parked?"

Ella hummed to herself. Marley had been her prime suspect. And now he was dead... She exhaled, her breath curling white in the cold air.

If Marley had been behind Bertram's murder, surely either he would have been thrilled... One less rival... Or if he regretted what he did, why not leave a note—why not confess?

And if Marley had nothing to do with Bertram's death...then why was he too dead?

CHAPTER 25

BECAUSE THERE'S A SERIAL KILLER?

TURNING ON HER HEEL, ELLA made her way around to the front of the imposing stone facade of the town hall, with the plan to enter through the main doors into the foyer. With any luck, the fire would mean the whole building had been evacuated, leaving her free to investigate Marley's office upstairs without interference.

Once inside though, Ella's hopes vanished. A mob had formed at the foot of the main staircase under the round window, bristling with anger, clutching cats, and arguing loudly with Robinne, who stood firm on the bottom step, arms crossed in defiance and not letting anyone pass. Among the crowd, Ella spotted a few familiar faces— Martha Chelton, the butcher's wife, and Bron the baker, who was wrestling with a particularly livid black-and-white cat trying to claw its way free. Several unfamiliar townsfolk, mostly clutching cats and kittens of various sizes and colours, were all talking over each other, their voices rising in distress.

At the back of the angry gaggle, one woman holding a fat ginger cat, caught sight of Ella and rushed her. "There she is—your ladyship!" She held up the cat. "Please help us! We need sanctuary!"

"Me first," a woman in an expensive-looking sea-green bonnet and matching cape elbowed her aside, hoisting a smart wicker basket in which several kittens nestled, each wearing white baby bonnets. "My precious babies are more deserving than your smelly moggie!"

"Whatever is the matter?" Ella asked, trying to catch Robinne or Martha's eye over the chaotic sea of swarming cat-ladies.

"The cat hunters!" Bron interjected, pointing in the general direction of the police station outside in the town square beyond, while the black and white cat in his arms yowled and tried to claw its way to freedom "No cat is safe!"

Ella's stomach lurched. Magic preserve! Of course—she should have realized. With Axel's bounty and Mr. Aladdin's wild claims about talking cats in Charmington, every rogue looking for easy money was sweeping up felines indiscriminately.

Could this day get any more troublesome?

"Robinne, please," Ella called, standing on her tiptoes, "I am more than happy to offer the cats sanctuary up in the tax attic. Can you please organise that?"

Robinne narrowed her eyes. "Why are you too busy? You haven't started on another *mystery* without me, have you?"

Ella opened her mouth to respond, but the cat ladies gave her no chance. They stampeded Robinne, who gave a resigned shake of her head, muttering, "Follow me," before leading them up the stairs like a sulky red-cloaked pied piper.

A familiar voice standing behind Martha said, "As I was saying, it's every citizen's responsibility, public safety. Someone has murdered the two frontrunner candidates to be mayor—and I intend to find out who."

Martha Chelton, adjusted her shawl, removed her long clay pipe, and jetted out a caramel-scented cloud of tobacco. "No, no, it's foolish to speculate. Besides they said poor Mr. Marley *drank* poison. Best leave it to Miss Cassidy," she said to the much shorter woman behind her—Marge, the town midwife, whom Ella hadn't noticed among the jostling cat-lady crowd.

Marge huffed, her blond curls jiggled as she stamped a foot. "I solved the old mayor's murder, last month!"

Ella turned sharply. "Excuse me? You did what?"

"I solved the murder of Sebastian, and I will solve the murder of Bertram and Marley too—someone is killing off *mayoral* candidates! That's no coincidence!" Marge nodded, her cherub cheeks aglow. She nudged Martha with satisfaction. "See, Martha! I can tell from Lady Ella's face that she agrees with me." The little plump midwife folded her arms and smiled smugly up at Martha. "Last month—I spotted the culprit, didn't I? That awful fellow who poisoned the mayor? Tell Martha, Lady Ella. You recall, I deduced as much at the mayor's tea party, didn't I? I said, *'That fellow has such a shifty air—does anyone else detect the distinct almond-like odour of arsenic?'*"

Ella clenched her teeth. That was most certainly not what Marge had *deduced* that day. "You *said* the mayor took two slices of the *dry* cake Sally *bought* and didn't touch your *homemade* macarons."

"Exactly!" Marge said triumphantly. "Shifty, like I said. You can't trust anyone who doesn't like my butterscotch macarons."

"THE NERVE OF THAT WOMAN!" Ella vented, under her breath, kicking out her long skirt as she strode down the town hall corridor towards the back stairwell. "*I'll solve this one too!*' Huh! As if she had *any* hand in solving the previous murders!"

Ella flinched as Tomcat, no longer wearing his goose hat, popped out from behind a large potted fern. "Ella! Please!" gasped Tom leaping back. "You nearly kicked me!"

"Oh! I am so sorry, I didn't realise what I was doing." She explained, "Kicking my skirt hem is a bad habit I had when my temper was riled when I was younger."

"I understand, but—hey! There's Doctor Hyde, we should tell him what we found out at the Haversham library."

Ella nodded, scooped Tomcat into her arms as the Doctor walked down the stairs. Though clearly busy, his eyes lit up when he saw the pair, and quickly ushered them to a quiet corner along the hallway among the fern display. "Mistress Charming! I am glad to have caught you. You know? About Marley?"

Ella nodded. "Indeed, and in regards to your request earlier, and though not conclusive proof, *someone* has ripped a Hangman's knot spell from a spellbook. Furthermore, all my investigations pointed to *Marley* as having purchased a red cravat, identical if not the tie itself as Bertram had on before the was knocked down."

The doctor looked perplexed, his brow furrowed. "And the tie itself? Have you tracked it down?"

Ella shook her head. "Not yet, but assuming Marley was the perpetrator of Bertram's demise, at least no one else should be harmed. I heard Marley was found with a glass of poison? Regret for his involvement in the affair?"

Hyde drew in his breath, a hand rubbed across his bald head. "Certainly, that is how it *appears*..." He looked about, as if to make sure they were not overheard. "I have yet to confirm that the bottle of poison, was poison—despite its being clearly labelled so—like it were stage prop—so carefully *placed* next to the body, if any actual poison was consumed, it will take an autopsy for that—"

"What's an autopsy?" Tomcat asked, peeking out from the folds of Ella's scarf.

"I'll tell you later." Ella shuddered and pushed his wee head back down, and lowering her voice, whispered, "Doctor, you're implying the cause of death wasn't poison, but something else?"

"You know my aversion to guessing, but considering the events of this morning, I must share a detail with you." Hyde stood back again, waited, observing for listeners-in. The hallway was not bustling with people and no one seemed to be paying their conversation any heed. He placed a deliberate hand to his throat. "Markings. Like before. *Identical.*"

Ella gasped. The tie had been used again!

Hyde nodded, seeing she understood, and added, "I strongly suspect the fire was lit to destroy the body, but it didn't take hold, there was more smoke damage than anything else." He stood straight and squeezed her shoulder. "I must go. I will let you know what my autopsy concludes." He bent down and looked her square in the eye. "Proceed with utmost caution, my dear lady. There may be a serial killer in our midst."

CHAPTER 26

HANSEL'S DISCOVERY

"**MY GOODNESS, WHAT A CONUNDRUM,** I thought certainly Marley was the culprit—for him to die really puts the cats among the pigeons—no offence."

"What should we do?" Tomcat hissed in Ella's ear. "Is there any point going to Marley's house now?"

Ella shook her head, already heading for the staircase. "A rogue once gave me some astute advice, *follow the money.* I shall do that now."

"Huh?"

"We'll snoop around Marley's accountancy office, see what we can find. Look for a shared link, some connection between the two deaths." She set Tomcat down on the stairs and gripped the handrail to climb, grateful that Goldi had treated her knees.

Tom padded up the stairs. When there was no one else in sight he said, "But there *is* a link—the death of two rivals—not to mention the playhouse curse."

"The playhouse curse is not a link!" Ella rolled her eyes. "We've been over this! There is *no Lady MacDeath* curse!"

Tomcat's fluffy white tail flicked. "Fine! Not a curse—but you can't deny the playhouse link."

Ella paused. "What link? Because Doctor Hyde said the poison looked like a stage prop? Do you think he was being literal?"

"I meant the actor Spalding. He's the link."

Ella frowned. "How is the actor son of his rival, linked to Marley? Never mind, explain later, we're nearly there now. Hush!"

A few minutes later, she pushed open the door to Marley's accountancy office.

The air hung heavy with the scent of burning, the once tidy office was blackened with smoke damage as Hyde had said, the walls and ceiling above the mantelpiece coated with soot. Sitting at Marley's grand wooden desk, Ella was taken aback to see Hansel's boyish face deep in thought, perched at the accountant's chair and flipping through a thick leather-bound ledger.

Hansel had soot smudged on his nose. Raising an eyebrow, he gestured with a sooty hand towards the fireplace, where there were several half-burned documents spilling out on the blackened hearth rug—perhaps the source of all the smoke.

Ella ventured over to peer at the handful of charred documents spread in front of the grate on what had once been a beautifully crafted Persian carpet. "You rescued these from the fire?" Ella asked rhetorically, the answer plain to see.

Tomcat likewise came and stood beside her on the ruined rug, his white paws causing the fragile documents to crumble. "You risked setting yourself alight!" Vampires were notorious flammable...

"*Nein*, zee fire was out vhen I arrived. Mr. Beau stopped it from spreading." He sighed. "I alvays admired Jacob Marley," Hansel said softly in his German-tinged accent, "For a human his bookkeeping vas...meticulous..." He slowly turned the folio pages over, the black ink numbers in their neat stacks and columns like orderly soldiers in rows. "I remember too, long ago, vhen Jacob's business partner died. By suicide. A bottle of poison drunk beside zee fire... Coincidence, no?"

Ella blanched and looked down again at the blackened documents. "What did you find?"

Hansel continued turning the pages, scanning them, while he rattled off what he had found in the grate. "Zere are some financial records, a failed patent application, a receipt of a Ravensthorpe cravat, and a large sum was paid to Mr. Beau..."

Ella and Tomcat shared a look. "So he did buy the tie!"

Hansel nodded as Ella approached the desk. "*Ja.* I am zinking receipt for clothes is strange zing to burn—as if to try and hide. *Ja?* Perhaps you are knowing zomzing about zat, I am not?"

"And the financial records? The patent application?"

"The application name was burned off zee patent, but it was declined." Hansel shrugged. "Worthless. As for zee other, zee payment to Mr. Beau was anonymous, but I am hunting..." He tapped a column before him. "Ah! Here. Meticulous. As Marley often said himself, zee numbers do not lie, I have found zee match. Marley paid Mr. Beau a large amount on behalf of zee Spalding family."

Tomcat's whiskers fanned smugly. He folded his arms across his chest and grinned up at Ella. "Told you there was a link to Spalding."

LEAVING HANSEL WITH INSTRUCTIONS TO look deeper into Marley's accountancy books, Ella and Tom set off. Tom had misplaced his goose-hat disguise when he ran to the town hall, but the shopping trolley was still in Ella's tax office.

They collected it and briskly trekked East to the Spalding's grand East Avenue residence. Last time Ella had been in the Spalding home was a month ago, when the former Mayor had been accidentally poisoned. And now, the mayor's son Bertram also passed away under bizarre and tragic circumstances. Some people had all the bad luck— Ella could understand why some were so swift to blame their change of fortune on curses. Life could be very unfair, and that was one of the reasons that made her so determined to see that justice prevailed.

Bertram's widow, Catherine was alone in the parlour when the maid servant announced Ella's arrival—after having helpfully assured her that it was 'no trouble at all' to place her ladyship's 'shopping' in the coat closet...

Feeling a little guilty at being forced to temporarily leave Tom hidden in the closet, Ella walked over to the ornate marble fireplace that dominated the parlour, where Catherine stood staring blankly at a beautiful clock under a glass dome on the mantle. Made of brass and gold, pendulum-like baubles spiralled at the foot of the clock, catching the light. It was not a Cluckoo clock, as they made in Charmington, but something perhaps from Avalon or farther afield.

"Bertie bought this clock for me on our first wedding anniversary," Catherine said quietly, without turning to acknowledge Ella's presence. "I've been standing here trying to recall his exact words, something about though paper was the traditional gift for the first anniversary, he wanted something to mark, not our past year, but our many years to come—our future time together, precious minutes..." She turned, her eyes red-rimmed, and her bottom lip wobbled. "I can't remember exactly! I can't remember what he said! It was so beautiful, he had a way with words! Why can't I remember?"

Ella placed her arms about the younger woman, who leaned into her shoulder as if to weep, but then quickly drew back. "Forgive me, Highness, I just—"

Ella patted the younger woman's hand, and held it gently. Few people these days called her by her title, but there were times she was reminded that she too was never far from her past life, no matter the passing of years. People may pretend they didn't know Ella's birthright, but they never truly forgot. If not for the separation of a few minutes, Ella would have been the Wyld Kingdom monarch, not Sibylla.

"Catherine, my dear, you have no need to ask my forgiveness, I am the one who should be asking yours, intruding upon you in this hour of heartbreak." She drew out her clean silk handkerchief and passed it to the younger woman, who dabbed her eyes and blinked rapidly.

Catherine appeared to give herself another mental shake and drew herself together. "How may I be of service, your highness?"

Ella felt a twinge of increasing sadness at the woman's coolness. It took Ella a second to remind herself that Catherine was probably in her mid-fifties now. Not the child of her memories, no longer the little girl who sang as she picked flowers from the palace summer garden. Perhaps being overly familiar would only cause her more pain. She would best be about her awkward business quickly and leave the poor woman to her grief in the comfort of her close friends and family.

Yes, to business then...

"I came to offer my personal condolences at your loss, I am deeply sorry for the tragedy that befell your cherished husband this morning..."

Catherine curtseyed and nodded, swallowing as if she might burst into tears again. "I am honoured you would come and tell me yourself."

"Alas, I must also intrude upon the memory of your beloved. You may be unaware that the accountant Jacob Marley has also passed away in tragic circumstances just an hour ago."

"Jacob!" Catherine's hand clasped to her lips, her eyes widened.

"You know him?" Ella frowned, surprised by the woman's emotion. "But, of course you must, Jacob and Bertram were political rivals..."

"Yes, that is, you see, to be honest," Catherine stuttered, blushing deeply, her cool facade crumbling. "Jacob and I were childhood sweethearts, until, of course, Bertram won my heart—it was nothing more than childish fondness, between us, Jacob and I, I mean. He was—his mother was a laundress, whereas I—I well." She broke off her babbling and drew a deep breath.

Ella smiled encouragingly, "You, my dear, were destined for *finer* things." Taking a gamble with her luck while Catherine seemed open to talking, and admittedly, a little frazzled, Ella pushed on. "It was exceedingly good of you to encourage your husband to use Jacob as the family accountant. Though political rivals, it speaks exceptionally well of your good breeding to separate politics from commerce."

"Oh dear!" Catherine blanched. "I would be eternally grateful if you didn't repeat that, the truth is Jacob was *my* accountant. Not my husband's. Bertram didn't know, but I gave Jacob money to help him set up, years ago—he was my childhood friend after all. I couldn't—I couldn't turn my back on him—but you know how people gossip. How they would, even now, misconstrue such kindness."

Ah! Yes indeed, Ella certainly did. And that was very interesting. So, if Catherine was Marley's client, not Bertram, then that meant the large amount of money paid to Mr. Beau came from Catherine. Whatever for?

"I have no doubt as your *good friend*, Jacob would have appreciated the charity shown to him when starting his business."

"You are so kind, Your Highness!" Catherine's reddened face suddenly paled as if she might faint. "And I wanted to apologise for my behaviour this morning, I—I know the doctor is a *good friend* of yours! It was wrong of me to accuse him of something so outrageous as stealing Bertram's tie—I am deeply ashamed."

Though surprised by Catherine's implication—Ella and the doctor *were* just friends—Ella seized on the moment. "Do not apologise, I quite understand, as did the doctor. Grief does strange and terrible things to even the most even-tempered and gentle souls... I took no offence. It was a very beautiful cravat. A Ravensthorpe if I'm not mistaken? A...ah, a wedding anniversary gift, perhaps? From yourself to your husband?"

Catherine wiped her face again with the square of silk, eyes lowered, and she folded it over in her hands. "No, from our son, Charles Spalding."

Ella turned about, casually, trying to convey nothing more than mild interest. "Ah, yes, I have met your son Charles, though his friends just call him Spalding. He's a very good actor, I hear. With a promising career."

Catherine bit her lip and crushed the handkerchief in her fists. "Yes, well, that is." She smoothed her skirts. "Bertie, my husband, didn't approve. I couldn't openly encourage Charles' hobby..."

The door opened and in strode the young man they were discussing, who bowed before Ella and then clasped his mother's hand.

"We were just discussing that handsome tie you gifted your father," Ella said pleasantly.

Spalding shrugged. "It was more his style than mine. I don't suppose I would have ever worn it." His mother's brow pinched, she looked confused, and Spalding added. "You recall, mother. I told you an anonymous fan, or whatever, left it for me at the theatre."

Catherine blushed, and uttered, "Yes, but certainly you *could* easily have bought it for your father."

"Ha!" Spalding retorted. "You'll have to forgive mother, Lady Ella," Spalding explained, "she's terribly embarrassed my acting wages barely keep me in crumpets and candles."

"I, for one, have always prized thrift as a virtue," Ella said, turning the conversation over in her head and wondering how she could bring up the subject of Mr. Beau and the money that it appeared Catherine herself must have had Marley pass on to the street lamplighter.

"Do you have any idea who might have left the gift? Mr. Beau perhaps? He was giving me a tour of the theatre this morning before it was shut down, and he seemed quite a fan of the arts."

Spalding rubbed his chin. "Funny you should mention that, the thought did cross my mind."

"Oh, really?"

"I saw Beau lurking around the theatre the day before, but following the announcement of the gas leak, I just assumed that was what he was up to."

Ella was watching Catherine's face when Spalding spoke and was surprised to see the widow flinch. A memory suddenly sparked in Ella's mind. Beau! Mr. Beau had *told her* this morning that Marley and Catherine had been in some relationship—how could she have missed that? Was Catherine *paying* Beau to keep his silence over an affair Catherine was having with Marley?

The widow suddenly clasped her son's arm, her eyes shut briefly then flashed open. "I have a confession to make! Son, please forgive me. I did it for you father—I know it was inexcusable but..." She took a deep breath. "I paid Mr. Beau a bribe to have the theatre shut down. There is no gas leak."

CHAPTER 27

DESTINY CATCHES UP

HAVING OFFERED HER CONDOLENCES AGAIN, and left the mother and son in peace to their shared grief, Ella collected the shopping basket—with Tomcat still squashed inside—from the coatroom and ventured back out into the cold.

Ella tucked a stray grey curl behind her ear as she pulled her hood up and cast a wary glance at the street behind them. No obvious fortune hunters loitering in the alleyways. No suspiciously eager passers-by staring at her shopping basket with a glint of avarice in their eyes. Still, she couldn't shake the feeling that someone was watching them, following them. If only she had her magic back! No one would have dared cross her when she was Haversham's prize pupil, top of black magic…

She tightened her grip on the duck-head shaped handle of Sally's basket, grateful they had the basket in which to hide Tom. "Magic preserve," she said under her breath, willing herself to focus on the case. "It was shocking to discover that Catherine paid Mr. Beau to get the theatre shut down. That must have been a hard thing to do, choosing what her husband wanted for their son's career when she herself knew how much her son enjoyed acting. Imagine having to choose between the wishes of two people you love." She paused at the street corner, waiting for a carriage to roll by, and frowned. "Father against son."

It reminded her of a time when it had been Ella against her sister Sibylla. Two twins. Born minutes apart. One designed to be queen, the other forgotten, cast off and forced to reminisce on the bad old days as if they had been better than they were…

From the shopping basket, Tomcat's head appeared, his ears twitching. "I've also been thinking about hard choices… We've assumed it was an accident that the cursed tie ended up on his father. We just took Spalding's *word* that he re-gifted the tie he received from an anonymous fan."

"Stay down!" She hissed but then carried on while considering his implication. "You're right. We can't rule out that Spalding could be lying about *how* he received the tie. But why? What would he gain?"

Tom's tail drummed against the insides of the basket. "What if Bertram was always the intended target? Um... I don't know if it's worth mentioning, but I've heard Robinne and Cassidy discuss that Spalding's dad wasn't happy he was an actor, like really unhappy—*I forbid you*—kind of unhappy..."

"Are you implying that Spalding knowingly gave his father a tie bewitched with black magic to purposefully harm him so he could be free to pursue the career of his choice?"

Tom tapped his front paws together tentatively. "Um. Yes."

Ella frowned as the thought took root. Marley had purchased the tie—that much they knew from the cravat shop. The real question was, had Marley or someone else cursed the tie with a Hangman's Knot spell before *or after* it found its way to Spalding? Marley's grievance had been with Bertram, not Spalding... at least, as far as she knew. If Marley's plan had been to throw Bertram off his campaign, it was a clever crime. Undoubtedly, Bertram would have withdrawn from the mayoral race to grieve his son. But then again... perhaps Bertram had been the true target all along.

Spalding and Marley *could* have been working together.

"Bertram wanted his son to follow him into politics, not pursue life on the stage," she mused aloud. "And Catherine's affection might be a source of a lifelong rivalry with Marley. So Marley and Spalding had a common enemy—"

"Yes. It all makes sense," Tom murmured, his fur bristling. "But I hate the idea of a son conspiring to murder his own father."

Ella tipped her head. "It is a remarkably dark thought—something more typical of my way of thinking than yours. Well done. I should have thought of it first. Perhaps my insight into the minds of Charmington's population is rubbing off on you?"

"Ugh. I'm not sure I'll take that as a compliment," Tom muttered. "I hate that it even crossed my mind. But I can't deny the evidence. We know Marley bought the tie, and I know the packaging was tainted with black magic."

Ella sighed. "People are rarely all they seem. Everyone has secrets. And sometimes, enemies." She glanced around again, her nerves prickling. A burly man on the opposite corner had been looking in their direction just a moment ago, but when she turned and glared, he suddenly found great interest in examining his own boots. Suspicious. She gripped the basket tighter and picked up the pace.

Tom shook himself, as if trying to settle his nerves. "So where to next? Shouldn't we find Robinne, before she finds out we've been running around trying to solve a mystery without her?"

"I believe we ought to have a few words with Mr. Beau. If we can get him to admit the theatre is perfectly safe, at least Nigella's life and the Pickford Players may be restored to normal. Beau might even be able to share some insight into the relationship between members of Spalding and his family."

Tom hesitated, his ears twitching. "I hope so—if Marley and the widow were just friends, surely he'd never risk harming her son. Even if he wanted to spite Bertram for stealing his old girlfriend, or whatever, then encouraging Spalding to be an actor seems just as plausible—unless..."

Ella narrowed her eyes. "Yes? Go on, Tom. You look like you've had another insightful thought."

Tom's whiskers twitched, green eyes blinked up at her. "It's just... What if Mr. Beau didn't have any such qualms about harming Spalding, or any of the Pickford Players? What if he just wanted to be paid for shutting the theatre down, no matter the human cost? As you said, Hansel revealed this morning that the maintenance staff haven't been paid in months."

Tomcat flattened himself into the basket as a group of children ran by, pointing and whispering.

Ella quickened her pace. Every passerby was a potential informant willing to trade their whereabouts for a reward. The bounty on Tom's head made their usual sleuthing more perilous than ever.

"Then let's get moving and find Mr. Beau. And keep your head down, Tom. I swear that man on the corner just started following us."

She wasn't sure if they were being hunted yet, but she wasn't about to take any chances. They were only safe while the Ahab didn't know what she looked like. But somewhere out there, Captain Ahab was lurking, waiting to get his hands on the great white cat.

BAKER STREET WHERE MR. Beau lodged was alive with noise, even before Ella and Tomcat stepped onto its cobbled path. The air rang with the shrill wail of a distressed woman, and a handful of nosy onlookers milled about, whispering to one another with great enthusiasm.

"This doesn't sound promising," Tomcat muttered from his perch inside the shopping basket, peering between the wicker work.

"Indeed," Ella agreed, quickening her step. The scent of damp stone and smoke hung heavy as a scattering of snow flurries fluttered and landed, seeping into her woollen cloak. The wailing grew louder as they reached the stoop of a narrow three storey terrace building, where a woman in a wildly patterned housecoat stood flapping her hands in great distress. "Oh! Oh, the horror! There's water everywhere!"

Ella barely had time to ask what was wrong before the woman seized her by the wrist and dragged her inside, jabbing a trembling finger at the ceiling. Water leaked steadily through the plaster, forming off-white, bulging spots. A thick, rhythmic drip came from the old-fashioned lamp, splattering onto a threadbare rug below. "Yes, well, technically I am director of rents and repairs, but—"

"No! Upstairs! Bath overflowing! And Mr. Beau—oh, poor Mr. Beau!" the woman wailed, gasping and pointing. "My tenant!"

Ella stiffened. "What do you mean—"

But before she could finish, Tomcat had already leapt from the basket and streaked up the stairs, vanishing from sight.

The landlady, still half-incoherent, flapped her hands toward the ceiling again. "Dead! Tripped and drowned in the tub!"

Ella's stomach lurch. "Magic preserve!"

Her mind raced through the possibilities, while the landlady stumbled bawling outside to be consoled by her neighbours, but Ella barely had time to think before a telltale heavy footsteps echoed from the street. Her heart dropped into her boots.

"Out of the way, important person, coming through," drawled an infuriatingly familiar voice. "What's all the fuss here?"

Axel.

The square-jawed, scowling sheriff removed his black tricorn as he ducked under the lintel and stepped over the threshold, his dark eyes locking onto her with a glint of glee.

"Granny Charming! Just the person I wanted to see!" Axel said, slapping his tricorn back on his head, his face brightening with the surprise of a man who had just found there was indeed a pot of gold at the end of the rainbow. "Where's your *priceless* feline?"

As if on cue, Tomcat appeared at the top of the landing, with Cassidy a step behind. Her composed, professional expression was in stark contrast to Axel's predatory smirk.

Tom blinked. "Oh, nuts."

Axel lunged.

Tomcat bolted.

Ella did the only sensible thing and flung her arms around the sheriff's torso. "Don't you dare—"

"Get off!" Axel snarled, shoving her away, he hot-footed after Tomcat out the front door and down the street.

Ella yelped and lost her footing, but Cassidy caught her. "Cassidy!" Ella gasped, steadying herself against the young guardswoman. "Tell me quickly—Mr. Beau, upstairs. Is he really—?"

Cassidy nodded grimly. "Dead."

Ella inhaled sharply. "Drowned? Or does it look like—"

"Like he was strangled?" Cassidy finished with a nod. "I could see there was something fishy even before Tom barrelled in—Beau is fully clothed. Even a smart red tie around his neck. Then Tom appeared and said we needed to go down stairs and fetch you." She blinked up at the ceiling. "I don't think you want to see what's up there though..."

Ella's mind whirled, pieces snapping together. "The cursed tie! Cassidy, listen to me—don't untie it! If it's still knotted, the spell is active!" She fumbled in her skirt pocket to draw out the remaining protective glove that Goldi had given her. "Wear this. You must *cut* the knot! You have a knife?"

Cassidy's eyes widened, but she gave a curt nod and took the sparkly glove.

"Take the cut pieces to Doctor Hyde for testing! He knows what to do!" Ella called out as the young woman dashed back up the staircase. "Don't touch the fabric—it's coated with black magic!"

Ella had no time to wait and see if her instructions would be heeded, because a deep voice barked from the front doorway.

"Black magic!"

Captain Ahab.

CHAPTER 28

DRAMATIC ESCAPE

"**WHO DARES USE BLACK MAGIC?**" Captain Ahab bellowed.

Frightened out of her wits, Ella bolted for the narrow threshold and collided with the wiry man. His single eye widened in shock as he grabbed for her arm. His wooden leg slipped on the icy step. For all his ferocity, he was a slender build.

Head over heels they fell.

"*Ooofff!*" Ella landed on her back, the wind knocked out of her, everything went black. Disorientated, Ella swept back her dark woollen cloak tangled around her head.

"Get off! Unhand me!" Ahab yelped as helpful souls milling outside the Baker Street residence rushed to assist. Swearing and cursing, impeded more by the over enthusiastic aid than his pegleg, he shouted at Ella, "Madame! I know you now!"

Ella was on her feet in a trice—*Thank the stars for Goldi's treatment of her knees!* A *whoosh* of rushing air and clatter of hooves filled her peripheral vision. A carriage!

The carriage door was banging open. A stroke of luck? A trap?

No time to think.

Ella lunged, grasping for the doorframe. Her boots barely found purchase as she flung herself inside.

The two occupants screamed—Ella braced for impact—but instead of a hard knock to the ribs, she plunged into a freshly laundered pile of fine ladies garments, a springy cocoon of silk dresses, sashes and fur coats. "Murderer! Fiend!" shouted one occupant's high-pitched, familiar female voice.

"It's me! It's me!" Ella cried fighting her way out of the topsy-turvy fabric she righted herself on the floor, popping up for air, her heart still thundering from her escape from the great-white cat hunter as the carriage wheels clattered carrying her away from the chaos of Baker Street. Magic preserve! That was close!

"Oh, thank goodness!" Mistress Fairweather exclaimed, clutching her fan to her bosom, the ostrich feathers festooned her bonnet bobbing back and forth, her relief as palpable as Ella's own.

Sam, the carriage's other occupant—and the twin sister to the orphan Sandy—helped Ella upright and onto a seat piled high with feather boas and fur hats.

The orphan was similarly dressed to her twin Sandy, in plush velvet, which reminded Ella that Sam and Sandy were being adopted by the good matron. To think it was only this very morning young Sandy had warned Ella and informed her that he was giving fortune hunters false directions—their luck had run out now. Ella shuddered, thinking of her near miss and Ahab's threat, *'I know you now!'*

Half-tangled within one of the lace shawls, Ella sat back into the padded seat of the bouncing carriage, part of her registering the carriage's rich interior—as plush, if not more so than her sister, the queen's own coach. Fairweather had certainly come up in the world. No wonder the matron was able to splash out on her charges with fine clothes. It was nice to see someone succeed after all the doom and gloom that changes in fortunes had spread across her town.

"You're not hurt?" Sam enquired, while untangling the lace shawl caught on Ella's bodice buttons. Sam's white pet rat, peeked out from her bulky lace collar. Like his young mistress, the rat was attired in luxury, wearing a very smart top hat, which he doffed before burying himself back in the young girl's neckline, presumably to sleep—or cling on—as the carriage careened round a sharp corner.

"I'm sorry for the unannounced arrival," Ella said, forced to hold onto the seat, "it was an emergency."

The matron laughed off the apology. "Think nothing of it—if only I can make an entrance half so dramatic then my stage career is assured! Thank heavens I decided against packing the tonic bottles at the last minute! They might have done you an injury, your ladyship— or worse, been smashed!" Fairweather continued, "Oh! Think of the lost profits!" She shook off the worry, adding, "I thought you were that horrid man, come to finish me off!"

Ella's thoughts went back to Ahab. She exchanged glances with Sam, who added, "He was in the orphanage! The one-eyed man! I caught him in the parlour, peering into the fireplace chimney!"

Ella gulped. It could not be a coincidence! Just last month, Tomcat had got himself wedged in the chimney breast of the orphanage. Magic preserve! Was Captain Ahab's tracking ability that good?

The carriage bumped and swayed as the matron regaled her own encounter.

"If I hadn't woken from my nap and screamed! I dread to think what he would have done! He fled out the window! And next door! Tell me, is it true? Beau's landlady was shrieking that Mr. Beau drowned!" The matron wailed and fluttered her fan and then pulled from her pocket a sample-sized bottle of her health tonic and swigged it down before breathing out a gin and mint laden gust of breath.

"The *MacDeath* curse is all Nigella's fault! Why did I ever listen to her? Oh, I'm next—I know it! I'm the leading lady! Marley succumbed to the flames! Bertram was trampled and now poor Beau has drowned. Hanging is the only fate left! What shall I do? Whatever shall I do?"

Ella raised a shade over the window glass and peered out into the darkening twilight Charmington streets. "Stay in public," Ella instructed the matron firmly, "where people can see you—perhaps the town hall. Plenty of people will attend the candidates' speeches. Not to mention Hansel and Gretel are there. They can protect you—and any Charmington citizen—from these fortune hunters!"

"Oh yes! What a magnificent idea," Mistress Fairweather cooed. Her ruddy cheeks once more aglow under the pale coating of makeup and powder. "Claude is at the town hall. I shall go under the pretence of aiding with his mayoral campaign! Then he'll be honour-bound and *have to* star alongside me and thus, the successful launch of my career is guaranteed! Oh your ladyship, that is a brilliant idea—I'm counting on it! However can I thank you? Have you sampled my restorative tonic? I will have the orphans deliver you a lifetime supply with a fifty percent off discount!"

"No thanks are necessary," Ella responded, wrapped up in her own darkening thoughts. Poor Tom! Where would he go? Her cottage out in the woods might be the safest place. But in town, where else would he go since her tax office was overrun by the cat ladies? Would he hide there among them—hide in plain sight? Or, even now was he within Axel's clutches?

Mistress Fairweather tapped the carriage ceiling with her fan and shouted, "Drive on! Northgate Square! Make haste!"

Ella slumped back in her seat as the bolting carriage swayed. Again and again she had been one step behind, too slow, too helpless to stop the killer loose in her town. Bertram was dead. Marley and Beau too.

Just as Fairweather had asked, Ella wanted to ask, *What shall I do?*

Ella shut her eyes. For once, she had no answers.

CHAPTER 29

SALLY REVEALS A SECRET

ELLA ARRIVED AT THE BACK door of Sally's haberdashery in very low spirits. She knocked and waited, glancing back over her shoulder, worried that someone might have followed—even with the dramatic escape in Fairweather's coach. She couldn't shake off the apprehension that Captain Ahab, skilled in the art of hunting, could still track her.

What a strange and terrible day. Mayoral candidates were dropping like flies and, with the bounty on Tom's head, no stranger could be trusted. Could even old friends be trusted?

Ella pushed the dark thought aside—in recent months she had learned a valuable lesson in trust and friendship from Tom. One could always turn to one's friends.

Cold wind swirled about as evening fell, Ella opened the back door and called out, "It's me, Ella. Anyone home?"

A muffled reply from Sally, somewhere inside, encouraged her to enter. She crossed the threshold—and immediately stopped short.

A peculiar sight greeted her. Tucked just inside the darkened hallway sat an old-fashioned pram, bulky and out of place. From within, a faint greenish luminescence glowed. Cautiously, Ella peered in. The pram was stuffed full of green wine bottles.

Revivor? Surely not?

Revivor was a banned substance extracted from dragons—long out of production and extremely rare. Yet, what other liquid casts a greenish glow? Ella picked a bottle and squinted at the label.

> *Lily's Health Tonic. Patented Limited edition! Enhances magical prowess! A delicious peppermint tonic containing pure glacial spring waters, direct from Wyld Kingdom—where every person is endowed with exceptional magical abilities!*

"Nonsense," Ella grumbled. "Marketing nonsense! This shouldn't be allowed." With a sigh, she placed the bottle back in the pram and ventured deeper into the haberdashery. The air smelled of lavender, beeswax polish, and the faint, musty tang of old fabric bolts leaning in the corners.

Sally was lighting the brass oil lamps in the cutting room. At the broad worktable, as well as this mornings detritus of white feathers and the usual array of silk flowers, spools of ribbons and hat forms, a thin young woman, dressed in smart black, but with a sickly pallor, was sobbing, and being comforted by young Olly, their vivid yellow ensemble a riot of sunshine next to the weeping girl in black.

"—and now I have to go door to door selling that swill!" The pale girl gestured to a sample bottle and two glasses filled with the eerie green tonic on the table. "It's so unfair! It's not even glacial spring— it's plain old well water!" She hunched over, sobbing into her hanky as Olly made grandiose promises about how many bottles Sally would buy.

Sally shared a strained look with Ella before saying, "Olly, dear, take your friend Penny into the kitchen. Make her some hot chocolate, then help yourselves to supper."

Once the younger ones vacated the room, Ella said, "You won't be buying any tonic, I gather?" She picked up the sample in the glass, sniffed the contents—and recoiled. The peppermint was like a slap to the face! And the alcohol fumes!

Sally pulled the stripy curtains, faded from years of sun, hung over the high back windows that flooded the room with light during the day and set about tidying the space. In the other room the clank of pots and chatter suggested the hot chocolate was underway. "Quite the opposite," Sally replied, her expression pinched. "I'll be saddled with purchasing that entire pram-load out in the hallway. I shouldn't wonder."

Ella frowned. "But...?"

Sally unbuttoned her polka dot cuffs and rolled back her sleeves. "But why buy it if I can't stand the vile stuff?" She looped an apron over her head and began the endless task of trying to sweep the feathers into a pile. "Because Penny is an excellent sales assistant— I'd hire her to work here if I could afford to—but more to the point. Because Mistress Fairweather *still* hasn't signed the documents approving my adoption of young Olly."

"I thought everything was finalised?" Ella assisted with collecting the stray feathers, gathering them into an empty hat box.

"Commerce," Sally returned tightly. Bemused, Ella arched an eyebrow and Sally lowered her voice to elaborate, "Ever since the attention her orphans received last month—you know, the special ones with the wyld magic, she's been fielding all sorts of inquiries from Avalon to Timbuktu!"

Ella stood up and placed the hat box full of feathers on an empty shelf between bolts of lace and cloth. "Are you saying Fairweather is trying to...feather her cap? Pad her nest a little?"

"A little?" Sally's tone turned acid. She waved a sharp hand. "I'm saying she is outright claiming their magical prowess is thanks to her tonic!"

Ella's stomach dropped. "She wouldn't let the children drink alcohol?"

"Of course not! But the ones with natural wyld magic—Sandy and Sam—they're being used as, what do you call it? Display samples!" Sally shot a glance at the kitchen, then all but hissed, "If Olly had magical tendencies, I have no doubt Fairweather would have taken them back!" The older woman's anger burst, and Ella strode forward and wrapped her arms around her friend as a slew of tears flooded.

"We won't let that happen," Ella soothed her friend, who wiped her eyes and pulled herself together, squeezing Ella's arm.

Sally pulled away, face pale. "I would *never* ask you to abuse your power—"

"I know, I know," Ella soothed, aware Sally had taken 'we' in its royal sense. "But, I'm sure if we put our heads together we can figure out a way together to get the adoption contract signed officially so Fairweather is out of your hair... After all, Fairweather's fortunes are on the rise. It's not even if she needs the funds."

"All Fairweather cares about is launching her acting career!" Sally grumbled. "Nigella has been bending my ear about it all month—and now the theatre is closed! Everyone is talking about the wretched curse!"

Ella sat Sally down at the cutting room table. "I have excellent news there! Mr. Beau's gas leak was a hoax!" Even as she relayed the news, Ella felt a sense of dread. Mr. Beau was dead. Dead in the bath, just like his ancestor before him. But who had placed the cursed necktie at his throat?

Despite revealing the theatre was safe, Sally's demeanour didn't brighten, instead she sighed. "The curse! Oh foolish Nigella, this is all her fault!"

"Whatever do you mean?" Ella pressed.

Sally leaned back in the chair and crossed her arms over her fancy gown. "I have known Nigella for years."

"Yes, as have I." Ella nodded. "She's a competent businesswoman and a superb actress. So?"

Sally gave her an exasperated look. "Have you ever noticed that, despite all her open auditions, somehow Nigella always ends up in the plum roles?"

Ella hesitated. "But... but this year, Nigella's recovering from a broken leg! She'll have to cast someone else as *Lady MacDeath*. She can't *hobble* around the stage."

Sally just shook her head. "How poorly you know her." She gestured to the feathers still littering the floor. "And I even let it slip this morning—Nigella commissioned me to make a goose costume for *Jack and the Beanstalk*."

Magic preserve!

Ella leapt to her feet, clutching her cheeks in horror. "Nigella had no intention of putting on *Lady MacDeath*! Fairweather's debut won't happen! It was all a lie!"

CHAPTER 30

ELLA'S GOOSE IS COOKED

"**BUT WHY?**" Ella asked, standing up. "Why announce *Lady MacDeath* if she has no intention of going through with it?"

"Who knows?" Sally stood and trimmed the wick as the lamp sputtered. "You'll have to ask her yourself. All I know is, I have been making Nigella a custom-fit goose costume for the last fortnight."

Ella paced the cutting room. Warm light spilled from the flickering oil lamps, casting golden patterns over the tightly packed shelves lined with fabric bolts, spools of thread, and tiny drawers filled with glass buttons. The faint scent of lavender sachets tucked between ribbons and lace softened the tang of peppermint oil and gin.

After a moment, Ella smoothed her skirts. Whatever Nigella was scheming, she had more pressing concerns on her mind—Tom's safety was top of the list. Then there were the horrid events of the day, not to mention the state of the kingdom's finances—oh dear! And now to find out that Fairweather was bullying Sally, and worse— potentially abusing her position as orphan matron to auction off children.

Suddenly, the tramp of quick boot falls echoed down the hall and Robinne burst into the room. She pushed back the cowl on her red cloak and bent over to catch her breath. Her chest rose and fell rapidly, curls tumbling free from her hood. "Thank goodness! You're here!"

Ella's heart leapt into her throat. "Is it Tom?"

Robinne shook her head, her heart-shaped face pinched with concern. "Hansel needs to speak to you—urgently. Why? Has something happened to Tom?"

"I lost track of him—on Baker Street! Axel was chasing him!" She spun about, gesturing in the general direction of the police station, which was across the square from the haberdashery. "And now the most tenacious of the cat hunters knows what I look like!"

Sally fetched a feathered mask. "You'll need a disguise if you're going out!"

Robinne tipped her head in agreement. "Good idea, but here's a simpler disguise." She untied the strings at her throat and swept off her long red cloak, holding it out to Ella. "You take my cloak, I'll wear your black one. You go meet Hansel in the post office and I'll scope out the police station to see if Tom's been captured."

Ella nodded, swiftly exchanging cloaks with Robinne. The thick wool was still warm from Robinne's body, carrying the crisp scent of pine and chimney smoke."If Axel has him—then keep him there!" Ella said, causing Robinne to blanch until she explained, "Tom is safer under Axel's lock and key than anyone else's—Axel will want to rub my nose in it before doing anything else."

"Gotcha," Robinne conceded, escorting Ella out the backdoor and into the cold. They parted ways at the end of the alley, Robinne in Ella's black cloak swirling off into the night, her boots crunching on the freshly fallen snow.

Folding her cane down and tucking it away into a red cloak pocket, Ella headed for the town hall, joining the crowds of people likewise ambling there, holding aloft banners, chatting in excited tones, and stamping their feet against the cold. Oh! She'd completely forgotten. The mayoral candidates would hold their speeches any moment, and she had promised Sibylla that she'd be in attendance to oversee proceedings.

Thank goodness for Robinne's loaned cloak. Not only would it disguise her from Ahab, at least from a distance, it might well help her avoid being called up for the mayoral debates.

Ella joined the crowd and followed the flow of people entering via the side door, thinking it would be faster to go through the building to Hansel's office located on the far side. However, unlike on previous town events there were two guards manning the entrance, diligently checking everyone who entered. Their posture was stiff, hands gripping the pikes as they squinted suspiciously at each face in the queue. It was no wonder. The whole town must be on edge with the strangers stealing cats and no doubt rumours were spreading about the tragic deaths.

The guards were barking odd questions at anyone they didn't recognise. "What day does Betty discount her salmon pies?"

"Er...Tuesday?" came a hesitant response from a man.

"Ha! No, never!" the second guard shouted. "Everyone knows they're sold out before noon!" Promptly putting their foot to the stranger's backside, the guard expelled him from the queue, adding, "Entry is permitted for Charmington citizens only!"

"What is the quickest way to Sutherby Auction house if you're travelling via donkey from the zigzag?" balled out the first guard and a few others in the line peeled off and Ella gulped, on finding herself at the head of the shuffling queue. The pikes clashed, locked in an X in front of her, barring entrance.

"No hoods!" said the first guards, her voice muffled and metallic behind the snout-nosed visor of the old helm.

"Show us your face, granny!"

Ella lifted her hood to allow them a quick peek.

"Oh—your ladyship! My humble apologies!" the second guard voiced, their tone switching from aggressive drill sergeant to polite and genteel. Both guards flipped back their helmet visors, revealing the actors Bob and Fishstix.

"I see last month's 'spear carrier' practice is being put to good use," Ella complimented the pair. "Keep up the good work, and—under no circumstances, allow entry to a man with an eye-patch and pegleg. He is extremely dangerous!"

Bob and Fishstix snapped off crisp salutes—clearly they had been practising that as well. "Marm, yes, marm!" Their visors clanged back into place and Ella strode on through the entranceway into the welcome warmth. Steam curled from her damp cloak, and the air inside carried the mingling aromas of baked goods, wet wool, and peppermint.

The bunting-strung foyer and corridors beyond the side entrance were crowded. Not only were the general citizens out to hear the speeches, there were families hovering over the radiators for warmth, while competing for their attention a salesman was touting a bar of Lynn's Fat Soap—*one bar lasts a lifetime!*

Further down the corridor, outside the ballroom, backers of various candidates were handing out flyers and touting banners and placards prompting their favoured mayoral candidate. A more unusual sight, dozens of people were carrying cats and dogs. Master Chelton, the large butcher and Cheapcuts father, had a raven on his shoulder that was mimicking a clock chime.

Ella elbowed through, trying to keep her borrowed hood up and head down, she navigated her way between the teaming townsfolk. She narrowly dodged a tray of hot pies, sidestepped a political debate in progress, and nearly collided with Baker Bron, who was carrying a hand-painted placard that read: *Save the cats! Vote Bron for Mayor!*

Looking up, Ella caught Marge's eye across the foyer. The little midwife was standing on a chair under a portrait of some former town dignitary. "Lady Ella!" Marge shouted, jumping off the chair and wading through the people toward her.

What now? Whatever it was, she had no inclination to stick around and find out.

Ella spun on her heel, darted away through the nearest doorway and found herself in the back of the main hall—right in the middle of Harold Harper's droning speech.

Ugh. Worse luck!

Ella eyed the distance across the seated audience to the far exit. Turn back? No time. Marge was fast approaching. Making a dash for it, Ella tiptoed through the people standing at the back of the hall, whispering, "Excuse me. Do pardon me. So sorry."

Claude was also seated up on the dais, awaiting his turn to speak while Harold Harper stood at the lectern, shuffling his notes in between repeating his catchphrase, "Tradition, tradition, tradition!" whenever he lost his place.

Seemingly finding his place again, Harold said, "You have no doubt heard the rumours of poor management, and foolish spending of taxpayer money! I can attend to this fact!" Harold said loudly. "Charmington used to be a respectable town, a town with a history!"

Which earned a few murmurs of "Hear! Hear!" from pot-bellied elderly members of the audience.

Ella gritted her teeth. But carried on weaving through the crowd. She had more important things to do than listen to Harold's moaning—when he was partly responsible for the trouble the town faced. Cutting all those maintenance jobs!

"My own hardworking and respectable daughter has been locked up under spurious claims!" He jabbed a hand at his breastbone. "I, who sought only to cut costs and to maintain financial order have been ridiculed and mocked!"

Ella stopped in her tracks. Spurious! Ha! Counterfeiting money was hardly respectable! "Ooh, lies!" she muttered under her breath, pushed back her hood, anger growing.

Harold caught sight of her and Ella gulped, realising her mistake. Magic preserve! Pride would be the death of her!

"Magic!" Harold blurted, his face reddening, his brown wig knocked momentarily askew. The audience turned heads, and seizing the opportunity, Harold stuttered, pointing his finger. "Hoarding riches while honest folk starve!"

What nonsense, Ella wanted to yell. Murmurs rose across the audience, confusion rippled across serious faces, unsure of whatever Harold was trying to say, but willing to listen. This was Harold's audience. Ella turned to leave.

One lady pointed, "And she ate my cat!"

"Mine too!" another cried.

"Ladies! Ladies!" Claude said, on his feet. His tall, handsome presence drew every eye. "My dear ladies and gentlemen, let us not disgrace ourselves. We are rational, intentional people. Let not our passionate hearts be sated with wanton speculation."

His velvet French accent, clear and commanding, flowed over the audience like silken butter. For a moment the audience wavered. Between sense and sentiment. And then Marge barrelled through the doorway.

"She's got a magic goose!" cried Marge, waving and pointing, cherub cheeks aglow, her pretty blond curls flouncing as she tap danced in excitement. "I saw it! A big, fat golden goose!"

Gasps spilled and people jumped to their feet. "A golden goose?"

"They lay eggs of pure gold!"

"Harold's right—That's hoarding magic and money!"

"Don't be ridiculous!" Ella retorted, drawing breath to counter the growing glint of greed in famished eyes, when Captain Ahab appeared behind Marge.

"Oh, blast!" Ella hissed, bolting for the exit.

CHAPTER 31

ELLA ON THE RUN

THE DOOR SLAMMED BEHIND HER, Ella picked up her skirts and ran along the corridor on the far side of the main hall, her plan set—she would lose anyone chasing her in the warren of basement tunnels winding beneath the town hall and post office.

How in the world did Captain Ahab get into the town hall? Ella wondered as she ducked into a narrow stairwell and pounded down the steps into the basement, grateful yet again for Goldi jolting her knees with the paid-fade magic earlier that day.

At the bottom of the stairs, Ella stopped, leaning against a stone wall that was warm under her touch. She caught her breath and listened. Was anyone on her tail? Not that she could hear. Good!

Now, which way? She had been down here just a month or two back. If she followed the main corridor she recalled there was a set of stairs that led directly up into the back offices of the post office where Hansel would be waiting for her.

She turned left then right, and was enveloped within the network of tunnels and halls that ran deep into the mountainside under Charmington.

Magic preserve! It was dark down here. Some corridors had gas lamps, but they were too dim and spaced too far apart to be useful. Ella unfolded her walking stick that she had tucked into the deep pocket of Robinne's borrowed red cloak and tapped the point twice to the floorboard in rapid succession. The craftsman mechanicals within the stick engaged and light flared from the tip in a wide pool, six feet or so. Inverting the stick so the light was at the top, she held it up to light her way and find a landmark.

Which way was the post office again? Hansel may have urgent news for her, but surely he wouldn't wait all evening! If only she hadn't become separated from Tomcat, his—or perhaps more likely the sense of direction he had temporarily inherited while his essence inhabited her cat Tilly—would prove invaluable now. Oh! There was a terrible thought. What if Hansel's urgent news was to report that Tomcat had been captured? No! That was unlikely, more likely it was to do with the kingdom's accounting books, or possibly even Marley's books. Ella thought to herself as she navigated the corridors.

Goodness. It was easy to become lost down here. Surely she should have reached the eastern stairwell by now?

Hmm… Had she gone down two flights instead of one? That would put her in the deeper maintenance levels, not the storage and document archives. Certainly nothing was familiar, the stonework was older, the ceiling lower and snaked with gurgling pipes overhead. Also the corridors were narrower, the air fuggy with the damp heat of thermal vents and somewhere the *blib-blib* water dripping on stone. Wait—was that the rush of water ahead? The air felt even thicker, almost humid.

Ugh. It was confusing, hot and noisy. There was a repetitive *thunking* sound that reminded her of a paddle steamer. She fossicked in the loaned cloak pockets, hoping to find a stick of chalk or something to mark her passage when she heard voices in conversation.

Fearing that it might be Ahab and Marge, she tapped out her stick's light and crept forward to peep around the corner. The odd water-thumping sound was drifting, echoing on the flagstone outside a stout door marked Pump Room. The metal door hung ajar, light was streaming from it. The pump room door suddenly opened fully, a roil of steam billowed out and Doctor Hyde and Goldilocks exited and both wiped their brows and then heaved the door shut with a clank.

Doctor Hyde had slung his black duster over one arm, his white sleeves rolled to the elbow. Goldi's bouffant sagged, damp strands of pink and purple hair clinging to her forehead.

"Should have brought a bottle of cool water," Goldi was muttering, fanning herself with hands as Ella made herself known.

"Thank the stars, it's you two!" Ella said, hurrying forward. "I was starting to think I'd be stuck lost down here forever."

"Mistress Charming," the doctor exclaimed, his frazzled expression lightening with a smile as Ella relit her walking stick to illuminate the corridor. "Do you have any news about the cursed-tie's whereabouts?"

"Some," Ella replied grimly. "Both good and bad. The cursed-tie has been found—and cut, too, breaking the spell so it can't harm anyone else. I sent the young guardswoman Cassidy to deliver it to you at the hospital for your testing and such as you required.

The bad news is I am no further in finding the culprit who enchanted it in the first place."

"That you have found and stopped the tie is excellent news," the doctor commended. "By coincidence, Mistress Goldilocks and I are well under way of narrowing down the source of the accidental poisonings. I doubt that the two are connected, but one should never rule out coincidence."

Ella's mind's eye darted to think of Ahab. Was it a coincidence that Ahab had been in both the doorway of Mr. Beau's house and the town hall above? Or something more?

Goldi stood up straighter. "Oh! That reminds me, speaking of enchantments, regarding Tom's predicament, uh—"

The little lady looked sideways at the doctor, but Ella interjected, "You may speak freely, the good doctor is a trusted friend and ally." His usually dour, hawkish features softened.

"It's not good news, I'm afraid. I found that book I mentioned in Sibylla's library and it observed that people, who underwent magical transformation, typically lost *all memory* of their time spent trapped within a mirror or beast or whatever."

"They lost all their memories? They must have retained some recollection, surely?" Ella found herself asking, an increasing edge of disappointment in her tone. Poor Tom!

"No." Goldi shook her head. "Seven out of ten cases lost their memory completely. And the few who were forced back into their bodies? They didn't even remember who they were *before* the switch."

Ella hung her head and shut her eyes, against the weight of the news. Poor Tom. This was worse than she'd feared. She took a steadying breath, forcing herself to focus. "Then we must ensure that he heals naturally, he will return to his human body in his own good time."

"About that...there was one other factor...And well, there was no case exactly like Tom's, so we can't assume it's the same, but...um. "Anyone who hadn't returned to their body within six months..." Goldi hesitated, shifting uncomfortably. "Well, I hate to say it..."

Ella braced herself. "Yes? Go on."

Goldi exhaled sharply. "They stayed that way. Forever."

Chapter 32

Hansel Strikes Paydirt

ELLA BLANCHED. "Stuck forever? As a cat?"

Goldi nodded. "A cat. Forever."

After a moment, Ella said, "I think it's best if I'm the one to tell him."

"If I might enquire?" the doctor asked, a dark eyebrow raised. "How long has Tom been a cat?"

"Six?—No, five! Five months!" Ella did a quick calculation on her fingers, and repeated it to be sure. "Yes, five!" Her relief was immense. She wouldn't have to be the bearer of that bad news at least. Poor Tom! How would he react when faced with Goldi's information? Even a kind and considerate young man as he would find it a vile medicine to swallow.

Oh dear! And that was even assuming that Tom hadn't been captured by Ahab. But wait, no! That fear surely couldn't be the case. For Captain Ahab was still tracking her! Surely that meant Tom was free—although perhaps he might have fallen prey to Axel's clutches! Oh dear! This day had started so simply and now it was falling to pieces.

Ella's thoughts were all a whirl. As if sensing this the doctor offered her his arm while Goldi directed the little party out through the warren of maintenance corridors and passageways. "What were you saying before?" she asked, leaning on the good doctor's steady arm. "About accidental poisonings?"

"Ah yes! It was our reason for venturing into the Pump Room," the doctor explained. "Mistress Goldi and I released a dye pod into several of the magical waste water traps—a different colour for each, and we came here to track if the dye was filtering through into any of the various water systems. No sign yet, which is good news! But it will take a day or more to be sure."

Ella looked to Goldi. "Not the drinking water, surely!"

Goldi shrugged. "No—the magical waste liquid traps and the drinking water pipes do not converge. If anything it will be some water fountain or the sluices for the drains. Something where water is recycled from rain catchment most probably. Unless there's a leak into the water table of course. But that's unlikely too."

"Unlikely but not impossible?"

The small craftswoman shrugged. "There's a bunch of extremely confusing blueprints if you'd care to join us in reading them? That's our next step."

"We were going to request Mr. Beau's assistance again," Hyde began. "Have you seen—"

Ella stumbled. "Oh! That won't be possible—poor Mr. Beau was the last victim of the tie! Oh, didn't I say?"

Hyde's dour expression pinched. "That is extremely unfortunate." He halted at the foot of the stairs that Goldi had led them to and brushed his hand across his bald head in a gesture of anguish. "I am loath to say it, you both know I hesitate in making outrageous claims, but three deaths by strangulation is a pattern I cannot ignore."

"It's the curse!" a voice boomed above from the stairwell. All three of them jumped.

A second later a white nose and whiskers appeared between the railing above.

"Tom!" Ella gasped, clutched her chest and breathed in relief when "You scared us! Thank mercy you haven't been captured, I was worried!"

"Sorry!" Tomcat peered down from his perch on the landing. "Goodness, doesn't the stairwell echo! But Doctor, were you about to say the deaths are due to the curse of *Lady MacDeath*?"

Doctor Hyde grimaced. "I have a great respect for magic, and I defer any such assumption to these ladies..." He bowed to indicate Goldi and Ella. "From my perspective purely as a man of science, I was going to say that either Mr. Beau fell victim to his own weapon, or there remains a tenacious and relentless killer on the loose. We must remain vigilant and hope that until his true face is revealed, disabling the cursed-tie has at least removed his claws—" Hyde flinched and turned to Tomcat. "Oh, apologies, no offence."

"None taken," Tomcat replied, whiskers fanning, as they walked up the stairs to join him.

Once again on the ground floor, Ella had her bearings and she parted ways with the doctor and Goldi who were headed to the blueprint archive. If Tom noted the sympathetic looks of concern that Goldi and Hyde spared for him, he didn't bring it up as he trotted at Ella's side towards Hansel's office.

"I am very relieved to see you escape Axel's clutches," Ella said as she ventured through the desks and shelves of the quiet and unattended workers area of the post office.

Tomcat's ears twitched and dipped, as if deliberating about something. "To be honest, Axel did catch me. But I gave him a telling off—saying how I used to look up to him and all that." He tilted his cat's head backward to catch her eye. "Did you know, he hadn't made the connection? He didn't realise that the cat version of me was Tom April, the rookie guard that worked for him! Gosh, he got scared! Mumbling about people coming back from the dead!"

"I'm not surprised you frightened him," Ella said archly, tapping on Hansel's office door. She paused. "Just...how badly are we talking?"

Tom sat. "Pee badly."

Ella choked on her laughter. "He *wet* his trousers!?"

"Yip." Tom confirmed as Hansel wrenched the door open.

"Highness!" the blond vampire said impatiently, his youthful face creased with frowns. "At last! I vas about to hunt you down!"

"Never something one wants to hear from a vampire," Ella muttered glibly under her breath, her mood still jovial from Tom's insight into their big bad sheriff's reaction.

"Is *nein* laughing matter!" Hansel snapped, all but dragging her into the neat post master's office that he had taken over from Harold. Hansel stood on his chair beside the mahogany desk and gestured to several charred bits of paper laid out beside ledgers written in Marley's handwriting. "The patent letter of application—the declined one that was burned in Marley's grate!" Hansel said as Ella and Tomcat peered in confusion.

"Yes?" Ella said, leaning over the desk and surveying the blackened papers and immaculate double-entry bookkeeping journals with no trace of comprehension. "Do the numbers not add up?"

Hansel gripped handfuls of his hair. "Toxic elements!" he blurted. "The patent was denied because of trace toxins found in the samples. Toxins which could lead to accidental poisonings!"

"The patent for what?" Tom asked, tail and hackles raised.

But even as Hansel pointed to the burned cursive handwriting on the document, Ella knew the answer.

Mistress Fairweather's health tonic was far less healthy than the label suggested.

CHAPTER 33

DIPLOMATIC BLUNDERS

"LILY'S HEALTH TONIC ISN'T HEALTHY!" Tomcat said, his ears flattening on his head. "I've seen lots of people drinking that today."

"As have I," Ella responded, hands clamped to her cheeks. Her thoughts returned to the pram full of green glowing bottles in Sally's hallway. Oh dear! At least because of the alcohol content, surely no one was feeding it to children. But then again... She recalled the sickly pallor of the young woman in Sally's haberdashery, the sales woman. And come to think of it, hadn't there been a few peaky faces among the orphans at the theatre this morning?

"Well water!" Ella gasped. "Could that be it! Oh dear, the young woman I met at Sally said that the health tonic was made using plain old well water—what if all the orphanage water is sourced from that well. And what if that well itself is the source of the magical wastewater poisonings Goldi and Doctor Hyde have both been trying to track down?"

Tomcat looked aghast. "Which well?"

Ella shrugged. "I assume one on Baker Street somewhere."

Tomcat's whiskers bristled. "The Baker Street orphanage has a courtyard well!"

"I vill send Gretel to Baker Street," Hansel said, promptly jumping from the desk. "And she vill stop access to zee vell. Zen I will find zee doctor."

Ella nodded. Her mind's eye flitted across the memory of the glowing greenish bottles stacked in Sally house. At least Sally would be unlikely to consume any, having already proclaimed her dislike of it. But how many other bottles could be out there? Oh dear. "We will have to find Mistress Fairweather immediately."

From deeper inside the connecting town hall came the distant rumble of applause. Ella turned toward the clapping. "The mayoral candidates will be gathered for the final debates! Fairweather should be there to support Claude—and with everyone gathered I can address the townsfolk if I must."

Their plans set, the trio parted ways. Tomcat ran at Ella's heels as she bolted down the empty corridors, abandoned as the citizens of Charmington had crammed into the town hall to hear the final addresses before voting for the mayor began.

"You really think Marley kept the patent results from Fairweather?" Tomcat asked, keeping pace with her.

"I do," Ella said absently, but her mind was already elsewhere. She stole a glance at Tom as they ran, her chest tightening. The thought of him forgetting all of this—forgetting her—was one she hadn't let herself dwell on. But Goldi had been clear. Once he was human again, there was no telling if his memories would stay. Perhaps... perhaps she ought to find a way to make sure he remembered. But how?

"I have heard Mistress Fairweather mention the patent several times," she added, her cane tapping the floorboards as she walked. "Not to mention all her recent spending. The matron clearly thinks her fortune is assured!"

"Wait!" Tomcat urged, skidding to a halt as they reached the main door of the town hall. "Not through there—this way! Follow me!"

Baffled, Ella picked up her skirts and followed Tomcat along the gallery of portraits around the outer hall corridor. "What? Why?"

"Because you'll end up stuck at the back of the audience—no one will see you." He slid to a stop and jabbed a paw at an unobtrusive door. "There—through there! That door leads through to the foot of the dais."

Pausing to catch her breath, Ella leaned over. "Right you are. Thank you. I had best go in by myself—I don't want to risk your safety." A thought popped into her head. "Tom! You recall earlier, you had a brilliant idea about writing yourself a letter?"

Tomcat's ears dipped and he held out his fluffy white paws. "Yes. But no thumbs to hold a pencil, remember."

"Yes. But you can type, can't you? Go up to my tax office in the attic now and use the typewriters there. Then you can seal the envelope and give it to someone you trust. Cassidy or young Olly? Or post it to your acquaintance in Nottingham, Master Spicer, was his name?"

Tomcat's green eyes lit up. "That's a great idea! Meet you upstairs there after the debates. Okay?"

Ella nodded and waved him off. She steeled herself as he pranced off down the corridor. His fluffy tail held high. Goodness. Poor Tom. He was such an optimistic young man. Always making the best of situations... He really had brought a change for the better in her life. To think that he might not even remember her once he was restored to his human form...

Ella shook off her melancholy. She had no time to dwell on such misgivings—there were other pressing matters to attend. Inhaling a deep, fortifying breath, she steeled herself to face the crowds as inside the hall the waves of polite clapping and foot-stomping was interspersed with murmurs of rhetoric.

The last thing she wanted to do was interrupt proceedings. Especially after Harold's outlandish accusations.

Ella slowed her steps, pressing her fingers against her temples as she thought. It would be horrid if she was to be shouted down or ignored outright—Harold had already done enough damage to her reputation with his wild accusations. If she barged in, demanding attention, she'd look just as reckless as he did. No, she had to be measured, firm, and—ugh—diplomatic.

Ella placed a hand on the doorframe, her pulse drumming in her ears. The polite claps and murmured rhetoric inside made her stomach twist. This wasn't like confronting a handful of people in the street—this was the entire town, packed into the hall, waiting for their next leader to take the stage.

Diplomacy... She could do this.

She inhaled through her nose, straightened her spine, and smoothed her dress. She could do this. She had to.

◄━●━•━•━•━──

Ella slipped through the side door of the town hall, careful to stay behind the tall town guards stationed at the foot of the dais. The cavernous hall was packed, the air ripe with the scent of snow-damp wool and anticipation. Could she weave in unnoticed?

Up on stage, the candidates including Claude, Harold and Bron were seated in a neat row, each waiting to answer questions raised by the audience.

Bron the baker was standing, and sputtering his way through answering a question on the poor state of the old road through the forest amid sightings of dangerous wild animals. "—not a werewolf! And there are no werebears either!" he blurted, red-faced, glancing to his neighbours' faces, Martha, Chelton and Cheapcuts, in the audience as if fur support. Chelton the butcher's raven, still on his broad shoulder, began squawking, "Wolves! Bears! Fresh meat! Two for one!"

While the audience settled amid laughter and another town member stepped up to ask a question, Ella stood on her tiptoes scanning the audience. She spotted the bob and sway of Mistress Fairweather ostrich feathers in her outlandish gauze and lace hat, while seated beside her, Nigella was dressed to the nines in a white fur outfit, and surrounding them, a clutch of orphans scrubbed and dressed in their best sitting in disciplined rows. Perfect. A quick word with the matron, and she could be on her way—

A trumpet blared.

Ella flinched as every head turned in her direction. The castle guards had spotted her standing behind them and, deciding to follow protocol in the most mortifying way possible, had signalled the trumpeter up in the musician's gallery. An entirely unnecessary blast of the royal fanfare rang down from above.

"Oh, for goodness' sake," she muttered, her plan for discretion foiled as a smiling steward appeared at her elbow. "Ah, Your Highness, right this way—your seat is waiting."

And just like that, she was ushered up to the stage, deposited into an ornate chair positioned front and centre—perfect for viewing the audience, she caught sight of Dirk, Sally, and Olly, waving at her, but utterly useless for speaking quietly to Fairweather.

The waiting town member, finally given their chance to ask their question, crossed their arms tightly, lowered their head and mumbled something unintelligible before being asked to speak up. "I said," they repeated, leaning forward, "what, if elected, would they do about the alarming rise in cat kidnappings?"

A murmur of discontent rippled out, followed by "Hear! Hear!" And a general dissent at the number of foreigners in town.

On stage, Claude, the bookshop owner, stood to answer. He placed a thoughtful hand on his broad chest, his voice rich with a lilting French accent. "It is my deepest regret that I was not born here—but I assure you, under my leadership, no cat shall go missing without justice. Every feline shall be safe, cherished, and, how you say... adored."

A pause. Then the sighs came, ladies fans fluttering. Ella rolled her eyes. The man could recite the alphabet or count to one hundred, and still have half the town swooning.

The polite applause for Claude's answer faded and jangling as she moved, Willow stepped up to the podium, peering at the paper in her hands. "Thank you, ah, Mr. Claude," she said, clearing her throat. "Now, before we break for supper, I have an important announcement regarding tonight's menu. Beverages have been generously provided by Lily Fairweather and will feature a variety of her Health Tonic—"

Ella barely heard the rest. Her stomach lurched. Lily's Health Tonic—the very same batch Hansel had discovered to be potentially contaminated. A good portion of the town was about to unknowingly poison themselves.

She shot to her feet. "Wait! You can't—"

But before she could finish, the hall doors banged open with a thunderous crack.

Marge the midwife ducked inside, somehow avoided the guards and swerved up onto the stage, blonde curls wild, her hat askew, her blue eyes darkened with terror.

"Stop!" she shrieked, clenching a tonic bottle to her chest, she hip-bumped Willow aside to take control of the lectern. "Lady MacDeath is among us!"

CHAPTER 34

MARGE PLAYS SLEUTH

"**DON'T TOUCH ME!**" Marge shrieked, flapping Willow away when she tried to calm the frantic midwife and Claude came forward to assist. "The Lady MacDeath scary-iller—serial killer is here!" Marge blurted, wafting gusts of peppermint along with slurred speech. "I know what I know!"

"Oh, good heavens, she's drunk!" muttered Harold Harper, scratching under his wig. He hitched a thumb at the guards to be about their duty and remove the drunken woman from the stage.

"Listen to me!" Marge shrieked, and she clamped onto the lectern.

Claude gallantly blocked the guards storming the stage. "Please! A man should aid a distressed woman, not manhandle her!"

The guards shrugged and muttered about just doing their job while Harold strode forward, now yelling, "Get that silly woman off stage!"

"There! Is, right—there! The killer!" Lurching about, Marge jabbed a wobbling finger at Ella while spitting out, "Lady Ella is a—one of them—a wolf! A wolf in a sheep! She murdered Mr. Beau in cold blood!"

A ripple of shock spread out.

Ella was too stunned to respond, as were most of the audience—apart from Harold, who suddenly relaxed and joined Claude in halting the guards while adding, "We should at least hear Marge out."

"Don't be ridiculous!" a voice shouted from the back of the audience near the main doors—Robinne. She pushed between a couple of citizens and stood up on a chair. "Ella is kind! She paid for the new hospital roof out of her own pocket!"

There were equal murmurs of agreement and dissatisfaction. "Easy when you have a golden goose!" a voice of dissent grumbled, which was shouted down by several people pointing out, "They don't exist—Merlin's *Guide* doesn't list them!"

Ella counted to ten in her head, both to allow herself more time to think, and also give the audience ruckus a bit of time to die down, before she addressed the drunken little midwife. "Well? We're listening. What is your...theory?"

"Ha! Theory!" Marge held her nose high. Took a quick swig from the tonic bottle. "Ha! Not a theory! I *saw* you at the office fire! And again at Beau's house!"

Ella refrained from rolling her eyes. "How astute—you *saw* me there! Well slap on the handcuffs and I shall confess my crimes!" Ella bit back further sarcastic retorts. "And aside from being *seen* there— what is your proof? Do you at least have a motive?"

Marge took an unsteady step towards Ella. "Because you need the money!" She waved her tonic bottle, splashing Claude and Harold with peppermint gin. "Everything in this town is broken! The hospital, the theatre—the lousy weather! You need the money to fix stuff! Because your goose isn't golden—it's cooked!"

Ella huffed out a breath, regretting she'd even thought Marge in such a state would have anything sensible to say. Even sober, the woman was nothing but a wanton spreader of gossip and malicious rumour. A bitter pill to swallow indeed! "Yes, well, we all could do with a few more pennies," Ella muttered, and was about to suggest someone escort Marge somewhere safe so she might sleep off her drunken state, when Harold's expression sharpened.

He straightened his waistcoat, stepping toward the crowd. "Marge does raise a valid concern!" he announced, seizing the moment. "I quite agree. The town has been run to ruins." He raised his voice and addressed the crowd. "A vote for me—Harold Harper, and I will ensure an end to wasted taxpayer money!"

"Repairing the hospital wasn't a waste!" Robinne shouted back, and in front of the audience Nigella and Mistress Fairweather surged to their feet.

"Who will repair the theatre?" Nigella asked, her clear stage voice raised above the noise. "Pickford Players Christmas production is a long standing tradition!"

"I came here to listen to Claude!" Fairweather called, waving her feather fan at Harold and encouraging her sickly orphans to 'Boo the bad man, children!' And then back at Harold, "Get off the stage you foul little paper pusher—you are standing in the way of true talent!"

Harold swore back and Claude was forced to intervene as the audience once more descended into chaos, arguing back and forth between candidates and citizens alike. "Ladies! Ladies, please!" Claude extolled, "While I value your support we have been over this—

I am retired! As I told Nigella, I cannot launch your acting career, madam!"

Fairweather looked aghast at Nigella. "But you told me that you'd sort it! That Spalding was the only hitch!"

Ella didn't hear Nigella's rebuttal as Marge shrugged Willow off as the baker tried to tempt her offstage with the promise of supper awaiting in the ballroom. "I haven't finished with her!" Marge rallied, sloshing the tonic bottle at Ella. "You and I aren't done!"

"Why don't we take this discussion somewhere private?" Ella encouraged while the guards and citizens' attention was trained on the mayoral candidates who were once more vying for their votes.

Marge shook her finger adamantly. "Oh, you would like that, wouldn't you? You're always telling people off in public!" She suddenly sat down on the stage and flung her arms about Harold's shins. "I'm not going anywhere! You jolly well deserve a taste of your own medicine!"

Despite nearly losing his balance with Marge clinging to his legs, Harold added, "I quite agree! My daughter was locked up on nothing but her flimsy testimony."

Ella was about to agree, a dose of her own medicine, spending the night in a quiet cell was looking all the more tempting, when a voice floated down from on high in the musicians gallery. "Doe—ray—me!"

And then someone sang out a single line with a familiar *Pirates of Penzance* tune, "I am the very model of a magic cat—a spectacle!"

Confused glances darted upwards. The bluster of arguments died on their lips as everyone looked up. What was going on? Who was singing?

Suddenly, something white pounced onto the gallery railing. A cat! Then rising up on its hind legs, it marched up and down, singing jauntily to the dumbstruck crowd.

> *"I'm on the run most everyday, in every way,*
> *because I am a mag-i-cal.*
> *A talking cat—imagine that—my value is most respectable!*
> *They see me here, they see me there, I drive them all hyste-ri-cal!*
> *I am the very model of a magic cat—a spectacle!"*

As the tune died away, the cat—Tomcat—saluted, jumped from the railing into the back of the gallery out of sight.

Someone said, "That's the talking cat!"

"It's worth an absolute fortune!" said another.

All at once the audience erupted, every person and their grandad surged toward the exits.

In a heap on the stage floor, Marge grabbed onto the lectern and hauled herself to her feet, but then swayed. "Think I'm going to be sick!"

"I shouldn't wonder," Ella said, and swiped the bottle from the midwife before she dropped and broke it. Ella stared at the heady peppermint gin of Lily's Health Tonic.

"A dose of my own medicine..." For a moment she was tempted to scold the midwife's over indulgence. Despite the misleading label, the tonic was far from medicinal and Marge had no one to blame for her state but herself. That couldn't be said for those wandering over to the supper. A large-scale accidental poisoning would be a tedious way to cap off an extremely ridiculous day!

Someone had to save the townsfolk from themselves, and as usual it looked like it was up to her.

Ella draped one of Marge's arms around her shoulder. Just as Robinne climbed up onto the stage. Robinne placed Marge's other arm across her own shoulder and hefted the little woman's weight.

"Did you see which way Nigella and Mistress Fairweather went?" Ella asked as they supported the tottering midwife between them.

"I saw them herding the orphans to the ballroom for supper."

"Good."

"Why?"

"It's time for the cool bit."

CHAPTER 35

BALLROOM WRAP UP

"ALLOW ME," SAID CLAUDE, SWOOPING in to assist Ella and Robinne, he gently scooped up Marge and followed them and Harold though to the waiting supper in the ballroom.

Inside, there was only a small number of milling people queuing at the buffet table, mostly Nigella's actors. Fairweather was off to one side scolding the salesgirl Penny. "What do you mean you sold the entire batch? I told you not to sell the special batch."

While Ella directed Robinne and Claude to place the drunken Marge at a supper table. Harold hovered around, casting spiteful glances at Ella, and muttering how Marge was 'under his protection' until her 'very important' allegations could be heard.

Across the room, Ella caught sight of the widow Catherine and Spalding escorting his mother, dressed in widow's black, to sit at a table that had been set aside to display Bertram's portrait.

Ella grabbed young Olly's elbow as the child darted by. "Why don't you gather up the orphans? It will be terribly boring while the adults chat. Go find the hidden lever in the portrait gallery and see where it leads..."

Word spread quickly and all the children skipped off and then Ella picked up a glass and tapped a spoon against it. All eyes locked on her.

"If I might have your attention. I shall be as quick as I can. I don't want to drag this out. We have all had a terribly trying day. My condolences once again, Catherine, Spalding." Ella paused and raised her hands and her voice. "For those of you unaware, we are all victims of a hoax. Mr. Beau lied about there being a dangerous gas leak, the theatre is perfectly sound."

"But why would he do that?" Nigella demanded, outrage etched on her features.

Catherine spluttered and cried into her black handkerchief. "It's all my fault! If I could take it back!"

Spalding placed a gentle and protective hand on his weeping mother's shoulder. "What's done is done," he said quietly. "Father forced you, and he has paid dearly for his meddling."

"Yes, it does seem Bertram has fallen foul of his own plot, but alas Catherine, you and your husband were likewise caught up in someone else's web. In some ways, we are all a little guilty, none of us can claim innocence. I confess I am partly to blame for reviving the ghost of *Lady MacDeath*."

"Ha! Knew it!" mumbled Marge, raising her head from Claude's shoulder.

"If I had not given Nigella a sixty-year-old newspaper to read while she was convalescing with her broken leg, a newspaper which reported the tragic events surrounding the last performance of *Lady MacDeath* then I doubt she would have even considered putting it on..."

"That's true," Nigella said, her tone full of sorry. "It was when you gave me the newspaper that sparked my imagination."

"But that reminder alone, Nigella discovering the *Lady MacDeath* play was just the beginning," Ella said. "There were two other crucial factors that steered her path. One, the theatre is struggling financially. And two, you have been facing constant pressure from a persuasive amateur, extremely keen to launch their career. Am I right?"

Nigella clasped her hands on her lap and cast an apologetic glance at Fairweather. "Yes, you have the gist of it."

"Amateur!" Fairweather intoned, deeply affronted, drawing up her bosom in indignation she turned her back on the director.

Ella ploughed on. "An amateur you were happy to ignore, until...?" She nodded, prompting Nigella, who sighed, and added,

"Lily offered to pay for the entire Christmas production provided she was given the role of leading lady."

"Oh!" cried Fishstix and Bob, both pointing at their playhouse director and then at the orphanage matron, as if something had just made sense to them.

Ella nodded as there was a ripple of contempt and mutters of cronyism and the disregard for the company's rules and such like from several of the actors, including Spalding, Bob and Fishstix.

Nigella's expression pinched with annoyance. "I was doing it to save the theatre! Pay your wages. It's not like sponsors are uncommon."

"Sponsors we can tolerate," Spalding growled, "But letting amateurs *pay* to secure a role? That's a crime against our noble art."

The actors glared at their director, and Nigella and Fairweather in turn glared back.

Ella held up a finger. "But there still remained an insurmountable fly in the ointment in getting the play underway. Fairweather *insisted* on choosing the male lead. A lead that refuses to come out of retirement because—? Nigella, will you force Claude to say it, or will you spell it out for everyone's benefit?"

Nigella pursed her lips, her arms wrapped tightly across her body. She shook her head and uttered, "Fine! Lily can't act! I tried and tried to steer her towards a panto! She has no talent for true drama. But as a horse's backside or moustache-twirling panto villain, we'd at least be able to put on a show."

"Oh! You foul villain!" Mistress Fairweather bellowed, surging to her feet, her ruddy cheeks red beneath the pallor of her powder. She clenched her fists. "This is outrageous! After all I have done for you! New wardrobes. New props! I paid for it all!"

"No, you didn't!" Nigella spat back, now on her feet and shouting down their sponsor. "You promise and promise to pay! But where is the money? I've had to put everything on credit!"

"Exactly," Ella said as the pair resumed their seats, but now Fairweather and Nigella sat with their backs to each other. "So, under increasing financial pressure, what does Nigella decide to do?"

"Oh! She gets the theatre shut down!" Fishstix cried, on her feet.

"No! She murders everyone to create a distraction!" cried Bob, caught up in the moment and applauding. "How very Greek tragedy of you! Bravo!"

"No." Ella said tightly. "Nigella announces that she wants to put on *Lady MacDeath*—believing full well that all you actors, being a superstitious lot, would simply refuse to be involved in the cursed play and after which Lily would be forced into performing a panto." Ella turned to catch Nigella's eye. "I know this is true because that's why you commissioned Sally to make the golden goose costume for *Jack and the Beanstalk*. You had *no intention* of *Lady MacDeath* ever seeing the light of day. Correct?"

Nigella waved a hand. "Yes! Precisely! I jolly well expected them to all throw a fit and refuse to perform this morning! Problem solved! But you wretched lot are too loyal!" She burst into tears and the actors rushed to her side and patted her head and arms and muttered also kinds of soothing words about loyalty and devotion to their most beloved director.

"A master stroke!" Bob commended, applauding his director. "Genius! You worked out how to save the theatre, and keep our reputation unsullied!"

"What?" Fairweather cried, yelling at Nigella once more. "But how could you? You told me *Lady MacDeath* would launch my career! I *believed* you!"

"What in the world does any of this play nonsense have to do with you murdering Mr. Beau?" Harold interrupted, glowering at Ella.

Marge's head popped up and she squinted beady-eyed at Ella. "Yes! Get back to the murder part! Don't forget who figured it out! Me! A killer lurks in our midst!" She burped loudly and sagged again, this time against Harold who gingerly pushed her over onto Claude's shoulder.

"I was getting to that." Ella smoothed her skirts. She looked up and caught Hansel's eye across the ballroom at the buffet table. He held up a little sausage on a stick. A salute to say, *Here if you need me.*

Ella cleared her throat. "I have gathered you here to refute the allegations made against me by Marge, but also because we must address the elephant in the room. There *is* a killer among us—not driven by a curse, but by *greed*. A desire to capitalize on a change of fortune."

She let that sink in. Several people shuffled in their seats, straightening their spines. The floor was hers.

"And it all began with a red tie purchased from Ravensthorpe. Supposedly a gift for Spalding."

The young actor blanched, his face already gaunt with the terrible circumstances of the day. Yes, indeed. He was a superb actor. But even he was unmasked in grief.

"Let's recap. So while ultimately Nigella *wanted* and *needed* the funds that Fairweather offered, to pay her company members their wages, she was banking on the actors to refuse to put on *Lady MacDeath*. She had in the meantime assured Mistress Fairweather that she would secure Claude's agreement to star opposite." Ella took a breath. "There remained one bottleneck to this plan. Spalding himself. What if he would not willingly step aside? Company rules dictated he was first in line for the role of male lead. Therefore our culprit decided to eliminate him."

Everyone gasped and turned, horror-struck towards Spalding, who leaned forward and placed his head in his hands.

Ella continued. "The morning before the play's announcement, an anonymous 'gift' arrived for Spalding—a red tie cursed with the Hangman's Knot, a spell designed to strangle its wearer."

Ella looked across at the eyes locked on her, the familiar faces, all deeply concerned.

"So you see, financial pressures and playhouse superstitions aside, the three tragic deaths today beginning with Bertram, followed by Marley and ending with Mr. Beau all stem from one individual's desire to have Spalding out of the way..." Ella let this information wash over the townsfolk and actors before continuing. "The question then is, who left the tie?"

"Ha!" Marge said, on her feet, pointing fingers at Ella. "You did! Case closed!"

"I quite agree!" Harold echoed. "Where is the sheriff when you need him?"

Ella ignored them both. One was drunk and was a toad. "Spalding, you told me that you had seen Mr. Beau lurking in the theatre."

"Indeed, I saw Beau yesterday," Spalding confirmed. "When I found the tie, I wondered if he had left it, and I admit I was a bit unsettled. I thought he was mocking me, giving me a tie like what my father would wear. But I guess he was just thinking up a good excuse to have the house shut down..."

Catherine the widow blubbered into her black silk handkerchief once more.

"That is what I deduced also," Ella said after a moment, giving the son time to console the mother. "But more than that, I suspect that Mr. Beau did in fact see who delivered the tie."

Those gathered gasped and drew closer, casting suspicious glances at each other.

"Furthermore, I suspect Mr. Beau saw the same person remove it from poor Bertram after he was supposedly struck down by the horse. And then when he put out the fire, he saw the tie yet again, this time on Mr. Marley. Beau guessed that it was no coincidence, and that foul play was involved. He may well have removed the cursed-tie from Marley, planning to keep it as evidence with which to confront the true villain. Or perhaps he had no idea the tie was cursed. Maybe he simply stole it—one act of vanity that sealed his fate."

"That's a lot of speculation!" Harold said, wagging his fingers. "You accuse Mr. Beau of theft when he's not here to defend himself! I agree with Marge's theory! After all, who knows more about black magic than you? You could have easily given Spalding a cursed tie!" Harold stood up and appealed to the audience. "What's to say she didn't drop it off herself? Let's put it to the vote, shall we?"

Ella folded her arms. "What motive do I have to get rid of Spalding?"

"Marge? Enlighten us," Harold spluttered and nudged Marge, but the midwife was snoring.

Ella let out a long breath. "Enough! While our culprit didn't intend for the litany of victims that have arisen, they must take responsibility. They intended most certainly to get Spalding out of the way, and though they did not place it around Bertram's neck, nor possibly Mr Beau's—but most certainly, they placed it around Marley's neck when he was in a drunken stupor, knowing full well what would occur. Didn't you, Mistress Fairweather?"

Chapter 36

The Killer Confesses

"Yes..." Mistress Fairweather said, sagging, and in a small voice, added, "I did it."

Everyone gasped.

"I...I just wanted rid of Spalding..."

"Why did you kill Marley?" Ella asked.

Fairweather sighed. "This morning after Bertram died, Marley told me my tonic didn't get the patent, you see. And I had run up so much debt... My future was being taken from me. I couldn't allow that."

"But black magic?" Harold huffed. "*You're* not capable. I'm not buying it. Marge, wake up. What do you say?"

"Funnily enough, Marley gave me the idea himself," the matron confessed, looking downcast at her hands. "His mother was a laundress at the old magical academy, and he told me how years ago he used the spell to kill off his business partner and make it look like a suicide." She shrugged at the irony. "He was terribly drunk at the time... I don't think he even remembered telling me the next day..."

Lifting her head, realising all eyes were locked on her in stunned silence, she surged to her feet. Everyone flinched. Held their breath, braced for attack.

Instead, Fairweather awkwardly kicked away her chair and bellowed, "Oh, woe!" She slapped her hand to her forehead, but then repeated the action, this time placing the back of her hand to her brow in a melodramatic showing of languish. "Hark! I am undone! Woe! Woe! The soldiers come!" She thrust out her bosom and launched into the final speech of *Lady MacDeath*.

About her, the audience reeled. Shook their heads, clearing the moment of shock at Fairweather's confession, their dazed wonder turning to artistic horror as Fairweather threw herself on the floor and rolled back and forth in-between stopping to breathlessly recite lines of Lady MacDeath's death throes. "A unicorn! A unicorn! My kingdom for a unicorn!"

Leaving the orphanage matron to her bizarre final performance, Ella waded through the crowd and quietly addressed the widow

Catherine and her son. "Thank you for being here. I know that was painful." She clasped Catherine's hands and squeezed them. "Go home now. Justice will be served. You have my word."

Tearfully, the widow just nodded, and moved away, but before he likewise followed after his mother, the tall actor said aside to Ella, "I feel this is my fault. If I had just, or maybe if Nigella had made me privy to her plans, or—"

"You said it best yourself. What is done is done," Ella said. "Go be with your mother. Blaming yourself, or questioning 'what if' will only trap you in time." She looked deep into Spalding's youthful eyes. "Believe me. I have been where you are. Lean on your friends, offer comfort in return. Don't hide, don't act that everything is fine. Just be yourself. Day by day it will get better if you allow it."

Blinking back a tear, the lad nodded and trailed after his mother.

Ella sighed, watching them go, but in her heart knowing that they would be all right. They had each other.

A distant wail of "Hark! The soldiers come!" pulled her back to the present. She turned, blinking, as if emerging from a fog of thought, only to find Mistress Fairweather sprawled dramatically across the floor. At some point, Marge the midwife had joined in, both women rolling about in a tangled heap of overacted misery.

With a grimace, Robinne offered her hand and helped the matron to her feet. Breathing hard, she thumped down into a chair, her ruddy face now looking queasy. Hansel hovered close by, as if she might make a sudden break for it. But judging from her greenish pallor, the orphanage matron wouldn't be doing anything of the sort. And perhaps, having held an audience enraptured with her swan-song performance, she was starting to sober up as her gin and tonic wore off and the consequences of her dark deeds were catching up.

After all, Ella reflected, once the show was over even the greatest actors must put away their costumes for kings and queens and return to normal life. Actors, too, were just people trying to make their way in the world.

Speaking of actors, most of the Pickford Players company had drifted over to partake in the buffet, several were blatantly piling plates high to take home—not that Ella could blame them. Tomorrow she would have to have a talk with Hansel and plan how they might best make use of what little funds the crown possessed that could be spent in supporting the townsfolk struggling to make ends meet through the long winter.

Ella observed too that Nigella and Sally were in the midst of their own brainstorming session about what was to be done for the Christmas play without a budget. They were laughing and bright eyed. And all in all, there was a sense of change in the air, as if indeed the play had ended and life once more would resume, flow in and gently erase the minutes of high drama, with the steady hours of pleasantly *normal* life.

Ella shook her head to clear her thoughts—magic preserve! Why had such peculiar poetic thoughts even entered her head? Clearly there was something very contagious about being in the company of actors. Perhaps they *should* be banned...?

She shrugged off that thought and walked back over to the matron who was fanning herself and taking deep gulping breaths. "Hansel, Robinne, will you help me escort Mistress Fairweather over to the police station where a warm dry cell awaits?"

Fairweather's eyes widened, panic darted across her face. She surged onto her feet and bellowed at Hansel, "This is outrageous! Keep your hands off me, little boy!" Then she turned to Ella, snarling, "This town needs me! I *pay* my taxes!"

Before Ella could answer, Hansel said calmly, but with deadly intent. "*Nein.* I have seen Marley's books—you do not pay your taxes." He bowed, clicked his heels and then grinned, his little white fangs glinting. "And I am *nein* little boy."

Fairweather gulped, let out a strangled little laugh, her fan stuttering mid-flutter. She took an instinctive step back. "Oh, pardon me. I must have misunderstood." She pointed using her ostrich feather fan—the feathers wonky and crushed from all the rolling— and gestured to the doorway. "This way, is it? A warm cell sounds good, thank you, very kind."

CHAPTER 37

HOME AGAIN—PLOT TWIST!

"**What a charming baby,**" **Ella** said loudly to Robinne at her side as the young woman pushed the bulky old-fashioned pram they had borrowed through the powdery snow on the forest path homewards.

"A charming baby?" Robinne replied, darting a glance into the darkness of the forest beyond the lamplight attachment of Ella's clever walking stick. "I think he takes after his father, but he has his mother's ears—eyes! I mean, eyes."

Inside the pram, Tomcat's ears dipped and twitched as he strained to listen to the sounds of the nighttime forest. Seemingly content, he snuggled back under the blankets. "You two are terrible actors, just go back to what you were saying about Goldilocks. No one is following us. That noise I heard a minute ago was only an animal."

Ella and Robinne exchanged glances. An image of Fairweather's outlandish and stilted performance of the *Death of Lady MacDeath* which they had both witnessed an hour ago in her mind. They crunched along the path in silence.

At last, Ella said, "And that's what Goldie found out. If we rush the natural order, either you'll lose part or all of your memories." She sighed. "I'm sorry."

"Oh," was all Tomcat replied to this solemn news.

"And what's happening with the orphans from Baker Street now Fairweather has been locked up?" Robinne asked as the silence stretched out.

"Ah—Sally, with Willow's support, is supervising everyone tonight and tomorrow while they are at Willow's bakery for breakfast, Doctor Hyde and Goldi are going to test the courtyard well."

"Do you think the well water could really have magical waste contamination?"

Ella shrugged, changing arms in which she held aloft the light. "It wouldn't surprise me. The laundering spell Fairweather used on the tie must have had an extra kick of something to make it so potent. And those glowing bottles of her tonic I saw suggested a magical algae of some kind. Time will tell. But we can be grateful her greed meant she didn't allow the children to consume the supposed health tonic."

"I'm sad for Sam and Sandy," Tomcat murmured from his baby disguise of blankets. "They were looking forward to being adopted…"

"Yes, well. I did have an idea there you see. Naturally it will be up to them, but I was wondering if I might adopt them…"

Robinne stared at Ella like she was crazy. "When did you start thinking that?"

Tomcat's face peered out from the pram. His whiskers fanned in a halo. "That's an awesome idea!"

"That's a crazy idea, if you're going to be adopting orphans—Your Highness—they can get in line behind me! I've known you the longest!" Robinne exclaimed mockingly.

"Oh, me too! Adopt me too!" Tomcat added. "I want a long princely name—what's yours again, Ella?"

Ella laughed at the pair of them as Robinne pushed the pram along. Gosh they made her smile. "Don't be silly—you're both adults. I can't adopt adults. And my royal name is Ella Discretion Fortitude Gertrude Charming."

""I want to be Tom Macaw Sage Charming! I've always liked Sage!"

"And I'll be Robinne Rebel Malcontent!"

"No, no," laughed Tom. "You should be, *Rebel Unicorn,* and I'll be, *Sage Unicorn!*"

Sage? Ella blinked. Her sister Cinderella and husband Richard had named their child Sage. What an odd coincidence… She pushed the thought aside as Robinne navigated the pram down the river bank and out across the frozen sheet of river ice that separated her cottage in its own wee island.

They were all laughing so much by the time they reached the cottage lawns, no one saw the man sitting on the front steps.

He stood up, swept back his hood and peered at the trio from his one good eye. "You have a Watson special ladies companion," he said admiringly as the light from Ella's walking stick illuminated his peg-legged figure. He asked, "Did you spring for the umbrella upgrade or the music box?"

Captain Ahab!

Dumbstruck, Ella and Tomcat's mouths hung open.

Robinne seized Ella's stick, and in one smooth motion, dive-rolled, opening the stick inner compartment as she did so. She landed holding the hidden blade to Ahab's neck. "No! The dagger!"

Ella's heart was still in her throat, unable to speak.

The man, however, grinned. He slowly held up his hands, and said, "There won't be a need for that, I assure you. Will there be, Tom April?"

Tomcat, at Ella's feet, pounced out of the pram and onto the porch steps. "Master Spicer?"

"Hello, Tom," said Ahab—Master Spicer—and he flipped up his eyepatch to reveal he had two perfectly good eyes.

"Robinne, that's my friend! Master Spicer, he's the cook at the orphanage I grew up in, in Nottingham."

Robinne cautiously removed the blade, but only after Ella managed a nod of approval.

"My humble apologies," said the small lithe man. "When I hadn't heard from Tom, other than receiving the odd letter—not in his handwriting I might add—and word had reached me that some terrible accident had befallen a new guardsman in Charmington, I thought I better come see for myself. Arriving, I sensed there was strange magic afoot, so I took precautions. Clearly, there was no need."

"How, how very good of you to check on Tom's well-being," said Ella, finding her voice at last. There was something familiar about Master Spicer. "I'm sorry, but have we met before?"

He smacked his forehead. "Of course! Forgive me, we both look so different. Constantinople! The sultan! Am I right? Your sister Arabella works for my former master. There was that thing with the flying carpet I made!"

Ella nodded, once again dazed at the realisation of who stood before her.

"What happened to your leg?" Tom asked as Robinne backed off and returned the walking stick to Ella.

"Oh this," Ahab—Master Spicer replied, laughing, and snapped his fingers. The pegleg dissolved in a shimmer of light and the fake limb transformed into a healthy counterpart matching his other leg.

"Whoa!" Tomcat cried, ears and tail vibrating with delight. "You can do magic! I never knew! Are you a fairy godmother?"

Spicer shrugged, and Ella coughed. "No, Tom. Master Spicer is a genie."

Tomcat's feline mouth split wide open in awe.

Spicer ducked his head. He shrugged again. "Anyways, I gotta run."

Ella suddenly remembered her manners. "Won't you come inside for some tea? Robinne makes delicious honey bark cordial."

Robinne pulled a face. "Promise I'll use a spoon, no knives involved."

But Master Spicer was already walking to the frozen riverside. "Another time please, forgive me." The air rippled in front of him, a swirling portal appeared. He waved farewell, stepped towards the light. But then halted. "By the way. The cat thing? Why the disguise?"

Ella swallowed. "It wasn't deliberate. An accident." She felt her ears turning pink as she blushed. Oh, how humiliating.

Tomcat stood on his hind legs and gestured to the pumpkin patch, where the jungle of vines and pumpkins lay coated under snow. "I wished on a star. And then my human body got injured. It's in that big pumpkin. Wanna see?"

"Yeah, I do!" The swirl of light behind Spicer suddenly collapsed and he strode over to investigate the plants, his voice full of curious admiration as he asked Tom a series of complex magical questions.

Ella was about to follow them when Robinne grabbed her elbow. "This is fun, but I'm freezing out here! I'm putting the kettle on, okay?"

At the same moment, Tom called to Ella, "Master Spicer said he can reset this. Okay?"

"Okay," said Ella to Robinne.

"She said okay!" Tomcat called to Spicer and darted back into the patch.

Reset...?

Ella dropped her walking stick. She spun about. "Wait! Tom! Your memories!" She sprinted to the pumpkins. "*Nooo!*"

—Boom!!!—fizzz—*whishhh!!!*

A sound. Then light. A swirling vortex sucking everything towards it. Then a bang! Pressure exploded outward.

A wave of magic roiling like a fireball.

The wave hit her with a clap of thunder. The force lifted her off her feet and blasted her backwards. She thudded onto the snow-packed grass.

...

What...?

Dazed and confused, Ella opened her eyes and blinked up at the stars twinkling in the dark night sky.

Why was she out here? Lying on the lawn in the middle of the night? Had she slipped and fallen?

Clutching her head she sat up. "Robinne?" For a moment she wondered why she was calling for her young neighbour. Robinne lived a mile away at the Crossroads Tavern. She wouldn't be here.

A noise, a rustling caught her attention and the pumpkin vines on the lawn unfurled. Goodness. When had they grown so big?

One vine reached out and stroked her head. "Yes, yes, I'm all right. I think I just slipped."

The vines ducked and swayed and suddenly Tilly padded out of the patch and bunted her head against Ella's knee. "Tilly! My sweetheart! Yes, I'm all right. What are we doing out here?"

She got to her feet. Magic preserve. Her knees! There was no pain. And gracious. Why was she dressed? Surely she had been in her dressing gown and night clothes a moment ago.

Gosh, her head pounded! And she had the weirdest feeling of déjà vu. She stopped and called out to the pumpkin patch. "Is...someone there?"

There was an odd noise, a soft implosion more than a crack, and a liquid whoosh. Then a man stood up from the middle of the pumpkin patch, a gooey substance covering his naked chest. He shook his head and thick beard, splattering bits of pumpkin guts on the lawn.

Ella was too startled to say anything for a second. But there was something oddly familiar about the bearded stranger. Could it be... "Richard?"

The young man combed his fingers through his beard. Steam was now rolling off him as the warm pumpkin innards hit the frigid winter air. "What a rush! Look at this beard I've grown!"

Ella clutched Tilly to her as the young man, whooped and shook his hair and beard, flinging pumpkin seeds everywhere. "Umm..."

The man looked down at his apparently naked body, hidden as he was in among the vines and said, "Ella! Can you fetch my clothes! On the sideboard! No wait, I need a towel!" He raised his arms and orange plant matter and goo slid off him. "Ella?"

Unsure what else to do, Ella turned away to fetch a towel. What in magic's name was going on?

"I'm going to tell Cassidy! It hit me just now! I have to tell her I love her!" he yelled at her back when she reached the foot of the staircase. "Wait—there's a towel and the clothes you leave out for Wulf in the barn!" There was movement and Ella heard her donkey braying in greeting, followed by an almighty splash, presumably the young man dunking himself in the water trough.

On the top step, Ella had to pause. The pain in her head was splitting. She gripped the railing. What had she been doing out here?

Something about a noise...? She'd heard a noise outside.

Shaking her head to clear it she bent and scooped up Tilly who meowed and bunted her face. "Yes, yes! You're hungry, I can tell. Let's sit by the fire and I will feed and brush you."

The barn door banged and she caught a fleeting glance of the man hopping to put his boots on as he crossed the ice, his shirt unbuttoned. His unkempt long hair dripped water. What was all the hurry about?

A fleeting memory surfaced. Tom April, the newest guard to join the castle, had stumbled into her yard. That was right. He was on his way to catch the midnight coach. Yes! She remembered now.

Stroking Tilly, and not quite sure why, but she felt a strong impulse to call out as the man disappeared into the night, "Goodbye, Tom April! I wish you all the happiness in the world!"

Then feeling foolish—after all she hardly knew the young man— Ella went inside and closed the door.

~The End~

Author's Note

Death Of Lady MacDeath is the last book in the series - if You have enjoyed the Wyld Enchantment Woods mysteries then Please write a review, or recommend them to a friend.

If you'd like to see more books written in this story world then drop me a line via my author website and let me know. Thank you!

About the Author

Kura Jane Carpenter is a New Zealand author and was the 2019 recipient of the Sir Julius Vogel award for Best New Talent.

When not writing, Kura enjoys convincing strangers that greyhounds make the best pets.

Web: **www.kuracarpenter.com**
Instagram: @kura.carpenter

Follow my Amazon author page for all titles in the series.
https://www.amazon.com/stores/Kura-Jane-Carpenter/
author/B0BGT43WSR